"I'm going to die!"

The chuckwalla bit hard into the end of Celina's nose. She fell back yelling, "Get it off! Get it off! ¡Quita me lo!"

Pellinore snarled and barked, kicking up sand and lunging at the lizard's tail. He ended up with Celina's shirtsleeve instead. Celina rolled around in the sand. "No, Pellinore! Patrick, get them both off!"

Patrick pushed Pellinore aside. He grabbed the chuckwalla and pulled. Celina let out a sharp yelp. "Don't!"

Patrick let up, but the chuckwalla didn't, its jaws still clamped tight.

"Get it off! Please!" Celina pleaded, her voice starting to quiver. "Please get it off! It's probably poisonous, or I'll bleed to death. I'm going to die!"

"Its teeth haven't even broken the skin," Patrick said. "There's no blood. Besides, it's gila monsters that are poisonous. Chuckwallas aren't. Don't worry."

Celina glared at him. "DON'T WORRY?" She was screaming now. "THERE'S A LIZARD BITING MY NOSE, STUPID!"

JUST CALL ME STUPID

◆◆◆◆◆◆◆◆◆◆◆◆◆◆◆◆◆◆◆◆◆◆

Tom Birdseye

PUFFIN BOOKS

PUFFIN BOOKS
Published by the Penguin Group
Penguin Books USA Inc., 375 Hudson Street, New York, New York 10014, U.S.A.
Penguin Books Ltd, 27 Wrights Lane, London W8 5TZ, England
Penguin Books Australia Ltd, Ringwood, Victoria, Australia
Penguin Books Canada Ltd, 10 Alcorn Avenue, Toronto, Ontario, Canada M4V 3B2
Penguin Books (N.Z.) Ltd, 182-190 Wairau Road, Auckland 10, New Zealand
Penguin Books Ltd, Registered Offices: Harmondsworth, Middlesex, England

First published in the United States of America by Holiday House, Inc., 1993
Reprinted by arrangement with Holiday House, Inc.
Published in Puffin Books, 1996

1 3 5 7 9 10 8 6 4 2

LIBRARY OF CONGRESS CATALOGING-IN-PUBLICATION DATA

Birdseye, Tom.
Just call me stupid / Tom Birdseye.
p. cm.
Summary: Terrified of failing and convinced that he is stupid, a fifth grader who
has never learned to read begins to gain self-confidence with the help of an
outgoing new girl next door.
ISBN 0-14-037954-1 (pbk.)
[1. Reading—Fiction. 2. Self-esteem—Fiction. 3. Friendship—Fiction.
4. Schools—Fiction.] I. Title.
PZ7.B5213Ju 1996 [Fic]—dc20 96-22955 CIP AC

Excerpts from *The Sword in the Stone* by T. H. White reprinted by permission of the
author, the Watkins/Loomis Agency, and the Putnam Berkley Group, Inc.

Printed in the United States of America

For those who teach—a noble profession. And for one teacher in particular—Debbie, who seeks the big picture, asks the hard questions, and yet never forgets to speak from the heart.

T. B.

Contents

JUST CALL ME
STUPID

Chapter 1

The White Knight

Mrs. Nagle's voice came across the table heavy with frustration. "No, Patrick. You're not paying attention. Look at the letters. Listen to the sound. W and H together says *wh*. You're a fifth grader, not a first grader. You know this. Cooperate for a change." She pointed to her mouth. "Look at my lips. I blow the air out through rounded lips. See, Patrick? Look at my lips."

Patrick Lowe did as he was told and looked at Mrs. Nagle's lips. They were bright red and very small, even though she had them sticking out in an exaggerated O-shape.

Mrs. Nagle blew air at Patrick and said the W-H sound over and over. It came at him in strong puffs, mixed with the smell of coffee. "*Wh, wh, wh, wh.* Come on, Patrick. The letters are here on your worksheet. Read the sound."

Patrick could feel the heat of Mrs. Nagle's demands as plainly as he could feel the afternoon heat in the small, windowless Reading Resource Room of Dewey Elementary School. The desert air outside had reached over one hundred degrees again, he could tell, even though it was late September and Tucson should be cooling down.

Mrs. Nagle had put in a request to the maintenance department for the air conditioner to be fixed over two weeks ago. "We'll be as cool as cucumbers in no time!" she had said with a smile. But the small fan that was only to fill in for a while still purred gently on her desk. It sounded like it was doing its job, but it wasn't.

Patrick slid over in his chair, even though he knew it would irritate Mrs. Nagle. It wasn't that he wanted to make her angry. He had to move away. It was that feeling again, as if a weight were pushing in on his chest and the walls were pressing in from all sides.

Mrs. Nagle scooted her chair closer to the table. "Read, Patrick," she kept insisting. "Look at the letters and *read.*"

Patrick looked at the letters, but it was no use. The air in the Resource Room seemed to be growing heavier, making it harder to breathe. He needed space and light. Mrs. Nagle leaned even closer, right up near Patrick's face. Coffee breath. He had to get away.

This time Patrick didn't slip farther across his chair, but across his mind. In an instant, he turned his thoughts in and fled. Mrs. Nagle faded. So did the Resource Room full of worksheets. And so did his old self. In his imagination he became the White Knight, just like when he played chess at home, riding off the board and across a sunlit meadow, lance held high, the light glinting off his shield—polished silver with a red dragon breathing fire—dazzling the cheering crowd that had gathered to see him joust.

"Pay attention, Patrick," Mrs. Nagle's voice cut in, each syllable as pointed as a knight's lance.

She was losing her patience. From far away on the sunlit meadow, Patrick could tell. He forced himself to blink back the White Knight and looked at Mrs. Nagle's mouth again. Now it was a firm straight line across her face, an angry line that quivered slightly.

Patrick wished he could make Mrs. Nagle happy. He wanted her to see that he knew the letters W and H, that he knew they said *wh*. He wanted her to see that he really wanted to read.

Because he did want to read; he had always

wanted to. He had loved books and the idea of reading before he started school. He used to sit with a book in his lap and pretend he was reading it, running his finger along the lines and making up the words he thought should go with the pictures.

He had been able to write his name when he entered kindergarten. By the end of the year he had learned all the letters of the alphabet. And he had been able to read words like STOP on the sign at the corner, and CHEERIOS on the cereal box. He had started first grade excited to learn more.

But then his new teacher had asked him to stand up and say the letter sounds in front of everybody. All of the kids had stared at him, and he had gotten mixed up. "That is a B, not a D," his teacher had said. "If you want to read, you must keep the sounds straight. You mustn't get them wrong."

Patrick had panicked. Dad had always said not to be wrong. "Get it right! Don't be stupid!" His father's voice so clear in his mind. "You spilled your milk; I knew you would!" All those times he'd made mistakes. "*Now* look what you've done!" Dad's face red with anger. "Wrecked your new bike? What are you, some kind of a klutz?" Liquor on hot breath. "N, Patrick! L-M-*N*-O-P!

Any idiot can remember that!" Fierce eyes boring into him, driving sharp points straight at his heart. "Get it right, will you! Don't be so STU-PID!"

Standing there in front of his first-grade teacher and all of the kids, Patrick had heard his father's words echoing in his mind. "STUPID! . . . STUPID! . . . STUPID!" He had felt his father's iron grip on his shoulders, the big hands shaking him so hard it seemed he would shatter and fall into a million pieces. "STUPID! . . . STU-PID! . . . STUPID! Get it right! Don't be STU-PID!"

Patrick had decided to say nothing rather than be wrong. He didn't want to be stupid. His first-grade teacher had kept on asking. The kids had kept on staring. But he hadn't answered.

Finally, after a month of asking, his teacher had called his parents. They went in for a conference while Patrick waited in the hall. He heard his dad get angry at the teacher. Then at home, after his mother went to work, his dad had gotten angry at Patrick, too. "Stupid!" he had yelled. He'd had a drink, then three, and gotten even angrier, so angry a rage had overtaken him and he had locked Patrick in the hall closet, yelling, "Maybe this'll teach you! DON'T BE STUPID!"

Patrick had been too afraid to tell his mother

later—how terrified he had been in that dark, suffocating place. He hadn't wanted his dad to get angry at her, too.

After that, reading had become the time to go down the hall to the Resource Room and Mrs. Nagle—for worksheets and drill after drill on the letter sounds. Every day he went. Every day Mrs. Nagle asked him to tell her what he knew. Patrick tried. But it all made him so nervous. He made mistakes. Mrs. Nagle asked again. Which made him more nervous, and led to even more mistakes. But Mrs. Nagle kept on asking anyway, until the weight of her questions bore down on his chest, and the walls of the Resource Room began to close in, cutting off the air and the light, just like when he had been locked in the hall closet. And Patrick had come to believe what his dad had said. He couldn't get it right. He really was stupid.

By the end of first grade, Patrick wouldn't pick up books anymore. The joy had gone out of them. Instead, he just drew the stories he thought *might* be between the covers—tales of knights and dragons and castles. Through drawing, he found he could escape into a world of his own making. It became his defense, his way out. And it still worked now, even after five years of Mrs. Nagle's stubborn insistence otherwise.

Mrs. Nagle. She meant well. Patrick knew that. She worked hard at helping him. Still, she was always pushing, as though she had some calendar that had his name on it, with the dates circled by the days on which she hoped he'd accomplish certain things. Lately, she'd been pressing for him to come to the Resource Room more often, even though Mrs. Romero, his regular classroom teacher this year, disagreed.

Patrick had overheard the two of them, Mrs. Nagle and Mrs. Romero, talking about it just yesterday. He had gone back for his lunch box, and overheard from the doorway.

"I know it's the policy of this school district to keep children with their age group," Mrs. Nagle had said, "but I still think Patrick should have been retained in first grade. He'd be doing better now. He needs more work, not less."

"Maybe if we took some of the pressure off," Mrs. Romero had suggested, "and let him learn to enjoy books again. In the classroom with the other children, he might show more interest in—"

"I think," Mrs. Nagle cut in, "I know what's best for Patrick."

The walls had begun to close in on Patrick as the women talked, the weight of their words pressing on his chest. He had slunk away without his lunch box, suddenly not hungry anymore. Behind the bike racks he had hidden in the bushes next to the school wall, drawing pictures in his mind of the White Knight charging off the chessboard into a real-life battle, charging across the sunlit meadow.

He had gotten away then, but now . . .

"Read, Patrick," Mrs. Nagle said again, and Patrick could tell that she was hot and tired, and today felt like Friday even though it was only Wednesday. "What sound does W and H make together?"

Patrick strained to say *wh*. But the sound got stuck somewhere between his brain and his tongue, and the air in the Resource Room seemed to grow even hotter. The weight pushed in on his chest until he couldn't get a full breath of air. And the walls. They were closing in again. The taste of panic rose in Patrick's throat. He had to get away. Now!

In desperation, Patrick grabbed his pencil and began to sketch on the W-H worksheet Mrs. Nagle had given him. A white knight—QUICKLY!—on horseback, riding into the meadow where he could breathe. Frantically, Patrick tried to draw his way out.

That's when Mrs. Nagle lost her patience. In a

flash of anger, she reached over and jerked the pencil from Patrick's hand, then grabbed his chin and forced it up so that he *had* to look her in the eyes. "Read!" she barked like an army drill sergeant.

For Patrick, it was as if his father had grabbed him again. He could almost smell the liquor, hear the closet door slamming shut. "Don't touch me!" he yelled, jerking out of Mrs. Nagle's grasp.

Mrs. Nagle went from angry to livid. "How dare you talk to me like that?" And for an instant Patrick knew that more than anything she wanted to slap him right across the face.

But just then the door of the Reading Resource Room swung open, and Mrs. Hollins stuck her head in. "Excuse me, Linda, but did you see the message from Mr. Gordon in your mailbox?"

Mrs. Nagle blinked hard. The anger slid from her face. A very tired look replaced it. She let out a long sigh, then carefully put another worksheet on the table. "Excuse me," she said to Patrick, as if nothing had happened only seconds before. "Please work on this while I talk with Mrs. Hollins." Then she got up and left the room, pulling the door shut behind her.

Still breathing hard, Patrick stared at the new worksheet. It seemed as if there was always one more where the last one had come from. Worksheets, worksheets, worksheets. The room was nothing but a long line of worksheets.

Outside the door, Patrick could hear Mrs. Nagle talking to Mrs. Hollins. Their voices were low, muffled sounds until Mrs. Nagle's voice rose in frustration. "*Another* cut in the budget? How are we supposed to teach if we have no money for supplies? How am I supposed to do my job? It's so hot in my room. Don't they know how *hard* it is to teach kids like . . ."

Mrs. Nagle lowered her voice to a whisper, a mumble through the door. But Patrick knew good and well what she said. He'd heard it before—"How hard it is to teach kids like Patrick."

Kids like Patrick. Kids like Patrick were what Mrs. Nagle was complaining about. Kids who lived across Verde Road in his neighborhood of small, frayed houses. Kids who were from families that were often only half families, fathers gone as his was now, or such a mess their fathers might as well be gone. Kids who had trouble in school. Kids who would never have what Mrs. Nagle thought nothing of: a shiny car with no dents, trips on an airplane, a big TV, things that smell new. Patrick knew *exactly* what it was like with kids like him. But Mrs. Nagle didn't. All she knew was her stupid worksheets.

Anger swelled in Patrick. He tried to hold it back, push it into the spot where he pushed most of his emotions. But he couldn't get hold. His face went red, his teeth clinched. In a sudden burst of motion, he swept Mrs. Nagle's worksheets off the table. He jumped up and lifted his foot to stomp on them, to show Mrs. Nagle just exactly how much he hated W-H.

But his foot was stopped short by the sight of the clean white backs of the worksheets. They had landed facedown on the floor. Their blank space seemed to call to him. Such a perfect place to draw.

Patrick checked over his shoulder for Mrs. Nagle. Her voice was back under control again, droning on and on in the hall. She was in no hurry to return to him, he knew. Not today, anyway. He was back under control again, too. No anger. He didn't care what she thought of "kids like Patrick."

Leaning down, Patrick quickly retrieved the worksheets, careful not to turn the W-H side up. He returned to the table, picked up his pencil, and began to draw. His hand moved smoothly this time, not propelled by fear. It floated over the paper in assured strokes, full of pleasure, not panic. His breathing returned to normal. The suffocating weight on his chest was gone. The room seemed much bigger, lighter, cooler. As Patrick drew, a smile worked its way onto his lips. He was where he wanted to be—in his own private world where no one, not even Mrs. Nagle, could reach him. "The White Knight is charging," he whispered, "charging out to fight a huge dragon!"

Chapter 2

Lupita's Pile of Beans

After school, Patrick took his time walking down the hall to the bus line. As usual, he wanted to be last. First in line, and Mr. Poole, the driver, would herd him to the rear of the bus. "Fill the seats from the back, kids," Mr. Poole would insist.

Patrick didn't like the back. It was noisy there, and that was where Andy Wilkinson liked to sit. Sometimes, depending on his mood, Andy would get weird and hassle people, especially Patrick. It was hard for Mr. Poole to see that kind of thing in his rearview mirror. Patrick took his time and got in the bus line last so he could sit up front.

It wasn't that Patrick was afraid of Andy. Just like Patrick, Andy was in Mrs. Romero's fifth-grade class. He wasn't any bigger or tougher than Patrick either.

Patrick and Andy even got along some of the time. Just yesterday at recess they had teamed up on the soccer field for a goal. Patrick had lofted a nice looping pass into the center. Andy had leaped up, his timing perfect, and headed the ball into the corner of the net. Goal! Andy had given Patrick a high five and yelled, "All right!" Some of the time they were almost like friends.

But a lot of the time they weren't. Today at recess Andy had yelled at Patrick for a bad kick during soccer, then broken in line in front of him at the water fountain. He'd also told Amy Taylor he didn't want to be in the same social studies group as Patrick. Patrick never knew what to expect—high fives or put-downs.

Some kids said Andy was crazy like his dad. Patrick knew all about crazy dads. Every now and then, when Andy was being nice, Patrick would think about asking Andy if his dad was still around, or if he had left like his own dad had, and never come back. But Patrick never asked. It was easier not to take chances with Andy.

Patrick got off the bus at his stop without a word from Andy. He started walking toward his house, trying to ignore the fierce afternoon sun burning into his shoulders. He was almost to the front walk and the shade of the lone mesquite tree when an all-too-familiar voice called after him: "Hey, Patrick, learn to kick the ball before you show up again for soccer."

Patrick turned to see Andy yelling out the bus window as it pulled away. "Or is that too hard for somebody like you?"

The bus rounded the corner onto Nathan Avenue, and Patrick couldn't hear Andy's other insults. He shrugged them off, and fished in his pocket for his house key.

But the front door was unlocked, and Patrick's mother was home. "Hi, I'm back here," she called.

Patrick crossed the small living room to the kitchen. His mother was scrubbing the sink. He stopped in the doorway and watched her work, her dark braid sweeping across her back each time she leaned into that old rust stain that wouldn't go away.

Ever since Dad had left, he'd taken to thinking of her as "Paulette" instead of "Mom." It wasn't as though he had decided to. It had just sort of happened over time. Thinking "Paulette" made him feel closer to her, as though they were partners as much as mother and son. She didn't seem to mind either, like some moms would.

"How was school?" Paulette asked over her shoulder.

Patrick put his backpack on the counter, pulled out a stool, and sat down. "I thought you had to work the lunch and dinner shifts."

Paulette stopped scrubbing and turned to face him. Though she was obviously tired—dark circles under her brown eyes, lines of fatigue on her face—her smile was bright. "Got a bigger break today. Thought I'd come home and get a few things done, see how you were doing." She glanced at her watch. "Gotta go back soon, though. So how are you doing? How was school today?"

Patrick shrugged. He hated that question even more than the "Who are your friends?" question. He knew Paulette was asking because she cared. She wasn't like Dad. She never yelled or shook him. She never called him stupid and locked him in the closet. Even after a conference with Mrs. Nagle, she always smiled and said she knew he'd do better soon. Still, especially after a day like today, Patrick wasn't interested in discussing school.

"It was OK," he said.

"Hmmm," Paulette said. She rinsed her hands, then dried them. "Had another weird customer in for lunch."

Patrick perked up. He loved to hear about the strange people who came into Lupita's Mexican Café, or the new joke Carlos the cook told, or what Lupita and Billy the dishwasher said to each other. They were always teasing.

Paulette leaned against the sink. "This guy wanted his burrito without a tortilla."

Patrick laughed. "No tortilla? But then it wouldn't be a burrito."

Paulette nodded. "That's exactly what I told him. 'But, sir,' I said, 'without a tortilla, a burrito wouldn't be much more than a pile of beans.' " She shrugged. "That was what he wanted, though. Billy said we should add it to the menu and call it Lupita's Pile of Beans. Lupita said the beans should go on top of Billy's head. Carlos heaped the guy's plate up three inches high and said, 'I hope he works outside.' "

Paulette laughed, and Patrick noticed that when she did, the tiredness left her face. She looked pretty.

"Oops," Paulette said, checking her watch again, "I have to get on back. But at least I work with nice people, and you never know who's going to come in and liven up the day."

Patrick nodded. "Yeah."

Paulette grabbed her purse and car keys off the counter. "I've got nursing class again tonight at the community college. I'll be home around ten." She leaned over and kissed him on the forehead. "Bedtime is at nine. Call if you need anything. You know the number." Halfway out the back door she turned. "I love you. Dinner is in the fridge."

"I love you, too," Patrick said, but the back door was already closed.

Chapter 3

The Kingdom

Patrick listened as Paulette started the car and drove down the alley toward Nathan Avenue. When the sound of the old Plymouth had faded away, he got up and crossed the kitchen to the refrigerator.

Cold air rushed out at him when he opened the door. Ahhh! He closed his eyes and just stood there for a moment. The air felt so good on his face, so soothing. He imagined it on Mrs. Nagle's face, soothing her, too. She would probably be easier to get along with when the air conditioner at school got fixed.

Patrick opened his eyes and surveyed the inside of the fridge: a bowl of leftover spaghetti covered with plastic wrap, jars of this and that, vegetables in plastic bags, cream cheese, pickles, a carton of eggs. Nothing very exciting.

Then he saw the leftover orange juice. Once a week Paulette splurged and bought a bottle of it fresh-squeezed at the fruit stand over on Fourth Street. Usually the two of them drank every drop for breakfast, but this time there was a little left. Patrick grabbed it, then shut the refrigerator door and took a sip straight from the bottle. The smell of oranges filled his nostrils. The chilled tartness of the juice rolled over his tongue. He thought about how great it would be to chug a whole quart without stopping. Fantastic.

But there was only this little bit left, so he drank slowly, small sips with time to savor in between, and looked at the photo Paulette kept on the refrigerator door with magnets—her and Dad before the divorce.

Charlie and Paulette Lowe, dancing, clowning around for the camera. They looked so happy together, Paulette smiling, pretty. It was a good photo. They looked as though they would love each other forever. Patrick smiled, even though he'd seen the photo a thousand times.

But then his smile faded. Why couldn't Paulette keep the picture in her room where he wouldn't have to look at it every time he needed something to eat or drink? Why should he have to remember? It had been two years since Dad had left for Montana or somewhere up north. He'd said he was never coming back, and he hadn't. He never wrote or called either. There was no chance for them to be a whole family again, as if they ever really had been. They were better off without Charlie Lowe. Why look at an old picture and wish things had been different? Why look at an old picture and dream?

Patrick turned away from the photo. He held the orange juice bottle up high, and looked inside as the last drops slid toward his mouth. Chug a whole quart without stopping, he thought. Yeah, that would be nice . . . someday. He put the bottle on the counter and walked out the back door.

Patrick's backyard was a small rectangle of packed dirt and dry weeds bordered by a chest-high concrete block wall. A clothesline ran the length of it on one side. The other was crowded by a one-car garage that could be entered from the alley. It was a dry, sunbaked place that made you want to squint . . . until you caught sight of the oleander bushes. A ten-foot-high hedge of them grew on the far side of the garage, between it and the block wall. The leaves of the oleander were dark green, and despite the hot, dry weather, the branches were still full of large white blossoms. The bushes looked like they belonged in a jungle somewhere, not in the middle of the Sonoran Desert. For Patrick, just looking at them made the harsh midafternoon heat seem less intense.

Patrick jumped from his back stoop and walked toward the oleander hedge. Once there he stopped, then checked over the wall on both sides of his yard to see if anyone was watching. Mr. Osman lived on the far side, but as usual seemed to be gone. The house on this near side had been vacant for a long time, ever since that old lady—Patrick couldn't remember her name—died. Nothing there but the big saguaro cactus, a prickly twenty-foot column of green, its one small limb near the top poking out like a fat nose. There was no sound other than a mourning dove cooing from its perch on a power line, songbirds in Mr. Osman's grapefruit tree, a distant truck on Verde Road. The coast was clear.

Satisfied, Patrick let his mind drift. He was the White Knight again, returning from battle, riding triumphantly across the sunlit meadow toward the castle gate. "The Kingdom," he whispered, parting some of the branches and ducking out of sight.

Between the bushes and the garage, Patrick had propped up an old piece of plywood at an angle, resting the high side on the sill of the garage window, the lower side on three stacks of concrete blocks he had found in the alley one day. He knelt and crawled under this roof.

The ground beneath was swept clear of twigs and leaves. Patrick moved over to an orange crate he'd laid on its side to serve as shelves. Miniature knights on horseback, drawn on cardboard and cut out to stand up, lined the bottom. Above them was a partially built model castle, also made of cardboard.

Patrick picked up one of the knights and inspected it carefully. He fished a pencil out of a coffee can kept behind the castle and added some shading along one side of the knight's shield. Carefully, he put the knight inside the castle walls, got another knight from its spot on the lower shelf, and placed it facing the first knight. Sitting back, he eyed the two, then made a slight adjustment in the first knight's position. Just right. He smiled.

Next, Patrick turned to a short table he'd made by placing boards on top of two concrete blocks. It stood in the middle of The Kingdom, and on it was a chess set, the white and black pieces already engaged in battle.

Sitting down cross-legged by the board, Patrick leaned close and examined the game. "So," he said to one of the black knights, "ready to fight, huh?"

He studied the board for a moment longer, considering. Think before you move, he told himself. Imagine the possibilities as far ahead as you can. It was what his father had taught him to do. For some reason there had been no pressure to always get everything right with chess. "There are a *million* possibilities," Charlie Lowe had said many times, smiling as he'd studied the board. "Chess is a *huge* puzzle!" They had played often, back before the really heavy drinking began. Patrick eliminated one move in his mind, thought some more about the possibilities, then made a decision.

"All right, you!" he sneered at the black knight. He moved his queen's white knight into a position that threatened the black one. It was a good move. "It's war!" In his mind he led his troops out of his castle toward the enemy, lance held high, the sun glinting off his armor and dragon-crest shield. Trumpets blared. Swords clanked as they were drawn from their scabbards. Horses whinnied. The battle cry sounded. Warrior voices rose to a roar. Patrick was there. He was the White Knight, and he was there.

"Hey, a saguaro!"

Patrick jumped, knocking over the chessboard

and spilling all the pieces. A dog barked. The shout came again.

"A saguaro! *My* saguaro!"

Patrick gritted his teeth as he looked at the wrecked chessboard. Just what was some loud-mouth doing trespassing on the vacant-house lot? And *who?* He crawled angrily over the spilled game and out of the oleander bushes.

Patrick stomped over to the concrete block wall and glared over the top, just as a tall, thin brown-skinned girl threw back her head, sending her long, shiny black hair flying, and shouted again. "*My* saguaro!" She grabbed the front paws of a little dog, and danced with it around the big saguaro cactus, her dark eyes sparkling with delight. "*¡Esta casa es mia también!*"

Patrick stood dumbfounded. He had picked up enough Spanish from the kids at school who spoke it to know what the girl was saying. *Her* house, too? What did she mean *her* house?

"We're finally back in Arizona!" the girl continued, now in English again, singing out her joy. She reached down and gave the little dog a hug. "And we've got a new family member, too! You, Pellinore! You!"

Patrick's frown grew even deeper. *Pellinore?* What kind of an idiot would name their dog *Pellinore?*

Chapter 4

Hey, Stupid!

The next morning at school, before the bell rang, Patrick turned the corner by the boys' bathroom and almost walked into Andy Wilkinson. Patrick started to sidestep around. But Andy sidestepped, too. "Hey, Patrick, read any good books lately?" he asked, his question lined with sharp teeth.

Patrick decided not to answer. It was what Paulette had advised him to do. She said that people like Andy said hurtful things to make themselves feel better; it was *their* problem, not his. He shouldn't pay any attention. So now he didn't. He tried to walk on past again.

But Andy wasn't in the mood to give up easily.

There were two fifth-grade girls from another class standing nearby, watching—Jenny Armstrong and Tracy Webber. Everyone knew Andy liked Jenny. He was always showing off in front of her, trying to impress her with how smart or athletic he was. Andy smiled at Jenny now, then stepped in front of Patrick once more, blocking his way. "Didn't you hear what I asked you?" he said. "Or did you forget how to listen like you forgot how to play soccer?"

Tracy giggled, but Patrick noticed that Jenny didn't. Maybe she thought *Andy* was the stupid one, not him. The thought brought a smile to his lips.

Andy saw the smile and turned red with anger. He grabbed Patrick's shirt and got right up in his face. "What are you smiling at, Stupid? Stupid! HEY, STUPID!"

The words hit Patrick like a fist. His mind filled with the memory of being shoved in the closet, the door slamming shut in his face. The school walls seemed to close in around him. He felt a suffocating weight on his chest. Panic shot up his spine.

Andy tightened his grip and pushed Patrick back, pinning him against the wall. "Anybody who can't read in fifth grade has got to be stupid."

Patrick gasped for air, trying to fight his way free. But he couldn't. The walls closed farther in. The closet door rushed at him, only to be stopped at the last second by an angry voice.

"Hey, leave him alone!"

Patrick, Andy, Tracy, and Jenny all looked down the hall. "Who's that?" Jenny whispered.

It took Patrick a moment to realize who was coming toward them. Her look was very different from the day before. Her mouth was set in a thin line rather than a playful smile, and there was fire in her dark eyes. But there was no doubt. It was his noisy new neighbor.

"Let go, you hear!" she said, aiming her demand straight at Andy.

Andy stared at this strange intruder, half questions dribbling out of his mouth. "Huh? . . . What? . . ." His grip on Patrick's shirt loosened slightly. It was all Patrick needed. He broke Andy's hold and shoved him away as hard as he could. Andy stumbled and fell to the floor.

"Whoa!" said Jenny, backing up. Tracy let out a nervous laugh. Patrick's new neighbor stopped short, looking back and forth between the two boys.

The look in Andy's eyes went from surprised to embarrassed to furious in less than a second. He sprang to his feet and attacked Patrick.

Patrick met Andy halfway. He didn't need a girl to defend him, especially not that loud-mouthed one. The two boys grabbed wildly at each other, locked arms, and crashed to the floor, rolling into Jenny and Tracy. Both girls screamed and tried to jump out of the way. Patrick's new neighbor yelled, "Stop it, you guys!"

They didn't. Andy swung at Patrick's face, hitting him on the ear. Patrick's head rang. He swung at Andy, then again and again, finally connecting to his shoulder. Andy clawed at Patrick's back.

The next thing Patrick knew, he was being pulled apart from Andy and up off the floor. Mrs. Romero's voice was sharp and clear in his ears.

"Stop this fighting right *now!*"

Patrick and Andy stood back from each other, gasping for breath. Mrs. Romero stepped between them. Usually, she was all smiles, her dark eyes sparkling, her words soft and full of encouragement. Not today.

"I will not tolerate violence as a way of settling disputes. Andy, this kind of behavior has got to stop. And Patrick, I'm surprised at you!"

Patrick looked away. Mrs. Romero was the nicest teacher he had ever had. She had a gentle way of making him feel OK. He didn't want her to be angry at him. He wanted her to know that Andy had started all of this. She would listen. Mrs. Romero always had time to listen.

But just then the bell rang. Everyone looked up as the doors flew open at the end of the hall, and kids began streaming in from the playground, talking, laughing, filling the corridor with echoing sounds.

Mrs. Romero took in a deep breath and calmed herself. When she turned back to the boys, her voice was firm, but even. "Get to class, you two. We'll discuss this during morning recess."

Tracy said, "But I thought it was a school rule that anyone caught fighting has to go to the principal's office and be sent home."

Jenny Armstrong scowled. "Shhhh, Tracy!"

Andy glared at Tracy as if he were ready to take a swing at her. Patrick looked at Mrs. Romero. It was true. That was the rule.

Mrs. Romero looked at Tracy and said, "Sometimes there are better ways to handle things." She turned and motioned for the boys to go on.

Andy and Patrick both let out sighs of relief, and Andy hustled down the hall. Patrick started to follow, but stopped when he saw his new neighbor walk up to Mrs. Romero. Just who did she think she was, butting into his business? He hadn't needed her help with Andy. What was she going to do now? What did she want with Mrs. Romero?

"I'm Celina Ortiz," the girl said, holding out a pink slip of paper. "Mr. Gordon gave me this note to give to you."

Mrs. Romero took the note and read it. "Another student," she sighed. "I've already got more than—"

"I'm glad I'm going to be in your class," Celina beamed. "Mr. Gordon said you love books."

Mrs. Romero looked up from the note at Celina's broad smile. She laughed softly. "Yes, I *do* love books." Then she motioned toward her classroom door. "*Bienvenidos*, Celina. Glad to have you with us."

Patrick couldn't believe it when Mrs. Romero squeezed another desk into the back of the class, right next to his. He ignored Mrs. Romero's formal introduction: "Patrick, this is Celina Ortiz. Celina, this is Patrick Lowe." He ignored the new girl's friendly smile also, even after she tapped him on the shoulder and said, "I think we're neighbors at home, too."

He already knew that. He also knew she had a loud mouth, and a stupid new dog named Pellinore, and didn't know when to mind her own business.

Patrick also ignored Celina later in the day when she read aloud from a thick paperback to Mrs. Romero, and Mrs. Romero said, "You read so well, with such feeling!"

Everybody stopped and listened, except Patrick. He figured they all thought Celina was really great, especially compared to him. He was almost glad when it was time to go to the Reading Resource Room. He was almost glad to see Mrs. Nagle, and worked hard for her on a new worksheet and with the drills. Mrs. Nagle smiled as if nothing had happened the day before, as if the air conditioner had been fixed, and told him, "Nice job!"

Back in the classroom Celina asked Patrick, "Where'd you go?"

But Patrick didn't answer. *None of your business!* he thought. He pulled out a piece of notebook paper and busied himself drawing another picture—the White Knight charging. *Keep your nose in your own backyard!* This time, the sharp point of the knight's lance was aimed straight at Celina.

Chapter 5

Keep Out!

Patrick walked to Lupita's Mexican Café that afternoon, even though the school rule was that if you weren't going to ride the bus, you needed a note saying you were getting home a different way. Patrick didn't have a note, but decided that he didn't care. He didn't feel like riding in the same vehicle with Andy, even though Mrs. Romero had made Andy apologize and Andy had even sounded as if he meant it. Celina would be on the bus, too. He'd had enough of her already. So he took off down Verde Road as soon as the bell rang at 3:10.

The afternoon was hot, the sidewalk like a furnace pumping heat up at Patrick's face. The busy

traffic on Verde Road made it seem worse, mix-
ing in the smell of car exhaust. Patrick's mouth
quickly became dry, his lips chapped. The sun
was white bright, and he had to squint. He walked
along feeling miserable, wishing he could move
to Alaska, trying to imagine big piles of snow.

But when he walked in the door of the café,
Paulette beamed, and he instantly felt better.
"Perfect timing!" she said. "Things are slow right
now. I can take a break. Sit at that booth by the
window." She didn't ask why he was there instead
of on the bus, just quickly got him a large glass of
lemonade. "It's so *hot* out there!"

"Any weird customers today?" Patrick asked
between big gulps of the lemonade. It tasted so
cold and good—maybe like melted snow from
Alaska.

Paulette slid in the booth across from him. She
smiled. "Just you."

Patrick rolled his eyes and took another long
drink. He liked it when Paulette teased. It made
him feel like teasing back. "Weird customer for a
weird waitress," he said.

It was Paulette's turn to roll her eyes. "I'm glad
you came by, Weirdo."

Patrick looked behind the counter and into the
kitchen. "Why? Need some help? Carlos and Billy
giving you a hard time again? Or Lupita?"

Paulette laughed. "No. Lupita's a marshmallow inside. She just acts tough. I can handle Carlos and Billy, too. What I need is for you to go home and get my nursing books for me. I forgot them again. I think I'm losing my memory."

"Getting old," Patrick quipped. The words just popped out of his mouth, and for a second he thought maybe he'd gone too far with the teasing.

But Paulette took a playful swipe at him across the table. "I know it's hot, but will you fetch them for your *old* forgetful mother? They might be beside my bed, on the nightstand, but I'm not sure. Find them and there will be another glass of lemonade in it for you."

Patrick finished off what was left of the cool, tart liquid. He stood and bowed—half in jest, half in seriousness—before jogging out the door toward home.

Once home, his cheeks flushed from the long jog in the heat, Patrick went straight to the refrigerator and stuck his head all the way in. He stayed there until his ears began to feel cold, then turned to find Paulette's books stacked on the kitchen counter. She had rushed right past them and out the door.

Patrick looked closely at the top one in the pile.

It was big and thick and had a slick paper jacket. No pictures. Lots of words. He reached out and slowly ran his fingers around the edge of the book, avoiding the large black letters of the title. It was about nursing, he knew that.

Paulette was always talking about her dream of being a registered nurse instead of a waitress. "Helping people feel better instead of lugging burritos." She would sit at the kitchen table, running her fingers over the books just as he was now, and go on and on about it. Her face would glow. The tiredness would fade away for a moment. "These books," she'd say, "are going to get us out of here." Then she'd reach out and give Patrick a big hug.

Patrick opened the top book on the pile. Before he knew it, he was looking at the bright white page covered with words. Halfway down, where a new paragraph started, one in particular caught his eye. What was it? *Re . . . Reg . . . Regul . . .* then he wasn't sure. What sound did an A with an R after it make? What was that rule Mrs. Nagle kept telling him? All of those rules she wanted him to remember. . . .

"Get it right! Don't be stupid!"

His father's voice sprung up from the page. In an instant the letters of the word blurred.

Patrick slammed Paulette's book shut, then

shoved the whole stack away. They fell off the counter, crashing to the kitchen floor. He whirled around, wanting to flee, only to find himself facing the photograph of his parents on the refrigerator door. Quickly, he covered his father's image with his hand. Paulette was left dancing by herself, so happy, so beautiful, smiling out at him.

Patrick turned back around. He picked up Paulette's textbooks, carefully wiping the dirt from the covers. He wanted her to do well in school, even if he couldn't. He wanted her to make it, to be better than Charlie Lowe had ever thought she could be.

Patrick grabbed his backpack and zipped the textbooks safely inside. He walked quickly to the garage, got his bike out, and jumped on. He rode fast down the alley in the direction of Lupita's Mexican Café, weaving around potholes, barely missing garbage cans, and completely ignoring Celina's friendly wave from over the wall.

When Patrick got back home, he went straight to The Kingdom. He was only halfway through the oleander bushes when he saw that a chess piece had been moved—one of his white knights. It only took a second longer to notice the note beside the chessboard.

Patrick knelt and picked up the small piece of

paper. Without looking at the words, he knew that Celina had written it. It had to have been her. Bothering him at school wasn't enough, huh? Now she had to sneak into his secret place while he was gone, mess with his chess set, and then write him a note all about it?

Patrick wadded up the note and tossed it in the bushes, then reached out to put his white knight back where it belonged. But something about where Celina had moved it stopped him. It was in a position that put the black king in check. And it looked as though the only way out of check would be to sacrifice the black queen. Dad had loved moves like that. "A perfect fork," he had called them, "sure to do damage either way you go."

The sound of a screen door slamming shut came from over the wall. Celina! Now she'd probably been spying on him, too!

Patrick jumped up and stomped out of the bushes. He glared over the block wall. There she was, just like he'd thought. She *had* been spying. He was about to yell at Celina to keep out of his stuff, his yard, his life . . . his words caught in his throat.

It was the look on Celina's face that brought Patrick to a halt. She was settling down on the shady back steps of her house, balancing a can of Coke on her knee, scooting over to make room for her dog Pellinore, and gazing at the book in her hand. As she started to read, her face glowed. At first, Patrick thought it was the reflection of light off the white page. But then he realized there was more to it than that. Part of the glow was the light, but part of it was some strange sort of contentment, too. He had seen it on Paulette's face when she read her nursing books. Now, there it was on Celina's face, too, and it stopped him.

It looked like it must feel so good to read without making mistakes, without the pressure, without things closing in. Suddenly Patrick wanted that feeling so badly that it make him ache. The ache was so strong, he had to turn away.

Patrick went back into The Kingdom. He looked once again at the chessboard, at the white knight where Celina had put it. The black king was still in check. The black queen would still have to be sacrificed.

He studied the board. It really was the best move, he had to admit. It was the perfect fork. Did Celina know anything about chess, or was she just lucky?

Patrick picked Celina's note out of the bushes and flattened it out on his leg. He looked at the words, struggling to read what she had written. He recognized a *you,* an *I,* and a *do.* He knew one

word near the bottom, too. C-H-E-S-S. *Chess.*
That word was on the box his game had come in.

Looking over the chess pieces again—at the
trapped king, the doomed queen, his white
knight—a question kept running across Patrick's
mind. Is she really that good? he wondered.
Really?

Chapter 6

The Sword in the Stone

The next day after school, Patrick sprinted from the bus to his house. He quickly let himself in, ran through the living room and kitchen, stopping only as long as it took to toss his backpack on the counter, then bolted out the back door. In seconds he was in The Kingdom, scooping up his chess pieces and board. He quickly set them up for a new game on top of the block wall, black pieces on Celina's side, white on his. White always moves first. Patrick pushed his queen's pawn forward two. Then he slipped back into the oleander bushes, where he waited in hiding.

It seemed like forever, but Celina finally came out in her backyard and began playing tug-of-war with Pellinore. She laughed as the little dog growled and pulled on an old towel. Yanking it free, Celina ran around and around the big saguaro cactus, Pellinore chasing her, jumping into the air and barking, trying to get the towel back. This went on for several minutes, until Celina stopped and said, "Whew, it's hot!" She let Pellinore pull the towel from her hand and drag it off to the shade by the back porch. "OK, *mi perrito,* it's yours." As she started to go to join him, she noticed the chessboard.

Patrick ducked farther back into the oleander bushes as Celina walked to the wall. "What's this?" she said to herself.

Through the thick hedge of dark leaves Patrick could see only parts of Celina's face, but the smile that crossed her lips was clear. She looked at the move he had made, then all around his backyard. "Hey, you want to come on over and play a game?" she called out.

The sound of Celina's voice so loud and so near made Patrick wish he had hidden farther away, maybe in the house where he could watch out the window. She was so close.

Celina tilted the edge of the chessboard up slightly and peered underneath. She searched the top of the wall, too.

Looking for a note, Patrick thought.

Celina called out again. "You know, come over and play face-to-face and all that, man-to-man . . . er . . . man-to-woman." She laughed. "You know what I mean."

Celina waited for a moment, then looked in the direction of The Kingdom. She put her hands up on top of the wall and boosted herself partway up, as if she were going to vault on over.

Patrick panicked. She would land practically in his lap if she jumped. What would he say? He'd been just as unfriendly at school today as before, and on the bus, too. He'd hardly even looked at her, except when he thought she wouldn't notice. How could he explain that despite all that, he still wanted to play chess with her? He thought of breaking out of hiding and running away.

But just as quickly as Celina had pushed up onto the wall, she changed her mind and let herself back down onto her side. She looked at the chessboard again and shrugged. Then she moved her black queen's pawn forward two squares to meet the white challenger. The game had begun.

And so Patrick and Celina played, never face-to-face, moves made when the other was not around. Patrick found that his new opponent was indeed good. Her move before with the white knight had not been luck. Every attack he launched she fended off, while at the same time countering with an attack of her own. Four days into the game, and they were dead even. Four days into the game, and they had each lost five pieces.

Patrick loved it. It was just like when he and Dad had had such great games, back before . . . It was nice not to be playing alone. No more imagining an opponent who could match his skill. He had one next door, even if she was kind of loud and had a dog with a dumb name.

But better yet, Patrick thought, he didn't have to talk to Celina. She kept trying to be friendly at school and on the bus. She'd even started playing soccer on his team at recess, despite the fact that Andy told her she wasn't good enough. "I can play!" she had piped back, and proved it. And after Patrick had scored from way out, Celina had slapped him on the back and acted as though they were old friends. But she hadn't come out to the wall when he was there planning his next move, even though he was sure she had watched from the window several times; he'd seen the curtain move. Even more important, though, she hadn't invaded The Kingdom again. She seemed to understand that it was his private world by the garage, and that he wanted to be alone there. She seemed to understand his need not to share that special place . . . until the next Friday, when the wind had picked up out of the west, and the oleander bushes swished and swayed. Without one word of warning, Celina climbed over the wall and ducked right into The Kingdom. "Hi," she said, and held out a piece of notepaper with writing all over it.

Patrick looked up from his half-completed drawing of a dragon, his mouth hanging open in surprise. He didn't even look at the note. He just kept staring at her.

So Celina told him what the note said. "You can't castle after you've moved your king forward to get out of check. Even if you move him back to his same place, you can't castle anymore. It's against the rules." Then she laughed. "I figured you just forgot, so I wrote you this note. You got my other one, didn't you? You know, when I told you all about exploring and discovering this neat place of yours. I just couldn't resist coming in. And then I saw the chess game, and . . . Well, Mom and Dad don't have much time for chess right now, since they both just started new jobs. That was all in that other note. But anyway, the wind kept blowing this note away—it's really wild today, isn't it?—so I just decided to come on over and—"

Celina stopped in midsentence when she saw Patrick's drawing. "Wow! That's a great dragon!"

Patrick glanced down at his work, then back at Celina, who moved closer, crouching for a better look. Not even Paulette had been in The Kingdom before. And yet, here was Celina blundering in uninvited for the second time.

Both anger and fear swept over Patrick. He could taste them on his tongue. He thought of fighting off this invasion, maybe even punching Celina. He thought of making a run for it, too. She was so close! He could even smell her. What was that? Banana? Yes! She must have eaten a banana for an after-school snack. Patrick picked up his drawing and held it to his chest. He didn't like bananas.

Celina leaned over and snatched the drawing out of Patrick's hands. Patrick sat in shock and watched as the banana-breath invader admired his art, turning her head this way and that. "I never can get dragons to come out right," she said. "You're good!"

Patrick's face turned red with embarrassment. He wasn't used to compliments, especially compliments from a girl. Yeah, run for it; get away. That was what he should do. If he could just get by . . .

"You know what?" Celina said, smiling. "This

picture looks a lot like I've imagined the Questing Beast!"

Patrick stopped. "The what?"

Celina looked directly into his eyes. "The
Questing Beast. You know, from *The Sword in the
Stone*. I told you I was reading that book in my
first note, remember? The Questing Beast is that
thing King Pellinore chases around all the time."

King Pellinore? So that's where she had gotten
the name for that dumb new dog of her's. She'd
named it after some king.

Celina began to dig in her pants' pockets. "I
keep trying to draw the Questing Beast the way
it's described in the book, but I just can't get it
right. Look, I'll show you. I've got some of my
drawings right . . ." She yanked a wad of folded
notebook paper out of her back pocket and held
it up, grinning triumphantly. "Right here!" She
quickly smoothed the pages out on the table.
"See?"

Drawings. They pulled Patrick in. He loved
drawings—any kind, anybody's, anywhere. And
here were pages of them, full of rough sketches
of some kind of a creature Patrick had never seen
or heard of before. Interesting! The head of a
snake—kind of—the body of a lizard—maybe—
except the back half looked more like . . . a lion?

"They just don't work, do they?" Celina said,

looking back and forth between her drawings and Patrick's face. "You're so good. I bet you could draw a great Questing Beast."

Questing Beast. Patrick rolled the name around in his brain. The more he thought about it, the more he liked it. Yeah, he liked that name. Questing Beast. So he said it. "Questing Beast."

Celina broke into a big grin. "Yeah! T. H. White is my favorite author right now. I love *The Sword in the Stone.* Mom let me read her original version of *Don Quixote*—you know, that story about the knight tilting at windmills. She said it's better to read it in Spanish; it lost a lot when they translated it into English. I liked it so much, she gave me a whole stack of books about knights and castles and everything, all that medieval stuff. And that's how I found *The Sword in the Stone.* It's an old book—1939 or something—and real English. You know, lots of words from England. But it's great, and funny, especially Merlyn. I like it so much I carry it with me all the time. See?"

With that, Celina pulled a paperback book from her pants' pocket and thrust it in Patrick's face. He recoiled, waiting for Celina to demand he read to her. His body went hollow as he waited for things to close in.

But Celina pulled the book back and quickly thumbed through it. "I love this part where Wart meets King Pellinore. Uh, where is it . . . yeah, page twenty-two . . . right here! Want to hear some? Just listen to this. It's such great reading."

The last thing in the world Patrick wanted in The Kingdom, *his* private place, was this banana-breathed invader reading a book.

But not waiting for an answer, Celina had already begun: *"There was a clearing in the forest, a wide sward of moonlit grass, and the white rays shone full upon the tree trunks on the opposite side."*

She spoke the words as if she were singing them, her voice full of feeling, caressing each sound as it crossed her lips. *"These trees were beeches, whose trunks are always most beautiful in a pearly light, and among the beeches there was the smallest movement and a silvery clink."*

Celina looked up at Patrick, smiled in obvious delight, then almost dove face first back into the book. *"Before the clink there were just the beeches,"* she read, *"but immediately afterwards there was a Knight in full armour, standing still, and silent and unearthly, among the majestic trunks."*

She paused, just long enough for the image of the knight in the moonlit forest to sink into Patrick's reluctant brain, then continued: *"He was mounted on an enormous white horse that stood as rapt as its master, and he carried in his right hand, with its butt resting on the stirrup, a high, smooth jousting lance, which stood up among the tree stumps, higher and higher, until it was outlined against the velvet sky. All was moonlit, all silver, too beautiful to describe.*"

Celina paused again. "Pretty cool, huh? Don't you just love good fantasy?"

Patrick didn't know what to say. He hadn't wanted to listen to this weird girl read a dumb story. But he hadn't been able to stop. Within only a few words, he had been pulled into that moonlit forest clearing as surely as if a big arm had reached out and grabbed him. He had *heard* the sudden "silvery clink." He had *felt* the presence of the knight sitting on the beautiful white horse, lance held high against a "velvet sky." Listening to Celina read was like walking into a dream—a dream that he had had many times before, yet never so full of rich detail.

"Read a little more," Patrick heard himself say.

Celina grinned, nodded, and did just that . . . for over an hour. First, she read the entire scene in which Wart—"the star of the story"—hears of the Questing Beast.

"Wart?" Patrick said. "What kind of a name is that? He must be pretty ugly, like a wart."

Celina simply said, "I don't think so." Then she went back to the beginning, "So you get everything straight." She read without stopping from page one to the end of the first chapter. Her voice rose and fell with the story, dancing over words that seemed impossible—*Summulae Logicales, chivalry, baize*—changing to strange accents, sometimes talking through her nose, as she switched to a different character. And even when she stopped to explain what this or that meant, or how it all fit together—"Kay is not really Wart's brother; Sir Ector is not really Wart's dad; that's important to remember; he's like an orphan, sorta"—she never lost the rhythm of the words she held in her hands. Patrick sat spellbound, lost in the magic of the book's world.

So when Celina finished the first chapter and Patrick asked for still more, she thrust the book at him and said, "Your turn!"

Patrick jumped back as if Celina had pushed a rattlesnake in his face. He swung his arm in self-defense, knocking *The Sword in the Stone* into the dirt.

"Hey!" Celina said with a sudden frown. "That's my book. Pick it up!"

Patrick's eyes went cold, darting around as if he were a cornered animal. Before Celina could get out another word, he blurted out, "I've got to go!" and scrambled around her.

"Wait!" Celina yelled. "Where are you going? I thought you wanted to hear more? It's your turn to read!"

Patrick jumped on his bike and raced down the alley, riding against the strong desert wind, rocks popping under his tires.

"What? . . . What did I say?" he heard Celina call after him. "WHAT DID I DO WRONG?"

Chapter 7

Friends

On Saturday, Paulette worked from 6:30 A.M. to 2:30 P.M., the breakfast and lunch shifts, instead of lunch and dinner. Patrick was up early to have breakfast with her before she left, stumbling sleepily into the kitchen and plopping onto his stool at the counter.

"You should be in bed, sleepyhead," Paulette said and kissed him on the cheek.

Patrick yawned. "And miss orange juice?"

Paulette smiled and got the new bottle out of the refrigerator. She poured two glasses full, just short of the rim, then carefully raised hers. "Happy weekend," she whispered.

Patrick raised his glass to click against Paulette's, and they both took a big drink. "Mmmm," Patrick murmured.

"I'll say," Paulette agreed.

Two pieces of toast popped up in the toaster. Paulette buttered them quickly and served them on one plate. She ate standing up, leaning against the counter. She did that a lot. Patrick always wished she would sit down. He'd only told her that once, though. She'd laughed and said that if she sat down, she might not be able to get back up. "And then what would I do?" Patrick had laughed, too, although they both knew it wasn't really funny. Now he didn't mention how his mother ate. She'd been up since 5:30, he was sure.

"Lunch at Lupita's?" Paulette asked.

Patrick nodded, his mouth too full to talk. Lunch at the café on Saturdays. Then dinner at home together—tacos! That was the routine. He liked Saturdays. No school. Lunch and dinner with Paulette. Usually they walked over to the ice-cream store in the evening, too. One scoop of anything he wanted. His favorite was almond fudge.

"See you around noon, then," Paulette said, finishing off her toast. She pushed the rest of her orange juice toward Patrick. "Think you can figure out something to do with this?"

Patrick grinned. "Probably."

Paulette laughed. Then she was out the door.

Patrick watched a couple of cartoon shows, got bored, and wandered out toward The Kingdom. Maybe he'd try to finish the castle if he had enough cardboard, or if not, ride down to the grocery store and check the trash bin for some. He ducked into the oleander bushes to find Celina sitting at the small table, Pellinore by her side.

Patrick stopped, half in, half out. Then he saw *The Sword in the Stone.* He recognized the drawing on the cover. Celina had it open in front of her. She began to read before he could turn and run.

"Chapter two: *A good while after that, when they—* you remember, Patrick, it's Kay and Wart out looking for the hawk, Cully—*when they had been whistling and luring and following the disturbed hawk from tree to tree, Kay lost his temper.*"

Celina stopped and looked up. "I thought you might like to hear some more." She grinned sheepishly, then turned to Pellinore and patted him on the head. He raised his chin and closed his eyes as she stroked his fur. "I know I'm trespassing," she said. She turned back to Patrick. "You're not angry like Kay in the story . . . are you?"

Patrick didn't answer. He wasn't sure how he felt. A strange mix of emotions flickered back and forth through him—fear, a bit of anger, and at the same time curiosity.

Celina continued to look at him, waiting for an answer.

He remained silent.

She shrugged and began reading again, this time a little faster:

"Let him go then," said Kay. "He's no use anyway."

"Oh, we couldn't leave him," cried Wart. "What would Hob say?"

"It's my hawk, not Hob's," exclaimed Kay furiously. "What does it matter what Hob says. He is my servant."

"I don't like Kay," Patrick interrupted. Curiosity had gotten the best of him, pushing fear and anger aside. He edged the rest of the way into The Kingdom and sat down cross-legged in the dirt.

Celina nodded her agreement. "Yeah, Kay's kind of a jerk some of the time."

Patrick scowled. "He doesn't even care about his hawk, and talks mean about Hob, too. I hate it when people act like they're better than somebody else." He reached over and retrieved a knight that had fallen off the orange-crate shelves, putting it back in front of the cardboard castle. "Paulette—she's my mom—says people sometimes treat her like a servant at the restaurant. It really gets to her, but she has to keep smiling and get them what they want, anyway. I wouldn't. I hate it when people talk to me like that."

Celina frowned. "Like that Andy kid. He's been saying mean things to me at school."

Patrick's mouth tightened. His eyes flashed. Andy had been in a bad mood a lot lately. One of the kids at school said Andy's dad was in jail. Still, that was no excuse for being mean. "In the story, does Kay always get away with giving Wart a hard time?" Patrick asked.

Celina looked back at her book, searching the page. "I guess there's only one way to find out," she said with a smile.

And she began again, this time with even more drama in her voice, acting out the book as much as reading it. Like the wonderful wizard Merlyn, who soon appeared in the story, Celina wove the words of *The Sword in the Stone* into a spell around Patrick, enveloping him as he sat on the dirt hideaway floor.

They got all the way to page forty-one and the end of chapter three—where Patrick was delighted to find that Merlyn and the talking owl, Archimedes, were going back to the castle with Wart—before Celina's voice gave out.

"I can't read any more," she gasped dramatically, holding her throat and slumping over onto the table.

A moment of panic seized Patrick. Would she ask him to read again like she had the day before?

She didn't. Instead she just sat back up, laughed, and marked their place using a twig for a bookmark. She looked around The Kingdom, then put *The Sword in the Stone* on the orange-crate shelf, leaning it up against the cardboard-castle gate. "The perfect place for it, don't you think?"

Patrick grinned and nodded, almost giddy with relief. He'd been able to enjoy a book, actually sit back and enjoy a story, without everything closing in. It made him feel . . . he didn't know what, crazy, happy, silly, goofy, to have done that. It made him want to get up and do something wild and fun. This girl named Celina Ortiz from next door was all right. She congratulated him when he did well in soccer. She had trouble with Andy, just like he did. And she played good chess. Despite her weirdness, he liked her. She was . . . well, sort of a friend. It had been so long since he'd had a friend. What should they do, two friends together?

"Hey!" Patrick almost shouted. Suddenly, he knew. "Let's ride our bikes down to the river and go exploring!"

Chapter 8

The Questing Beast

Down the alley they rode, then along Nathan Avenue, stopping only for the light on Verde Road, weaving around manhole covers, going fast, Patrick even riding with no hands. Pellinore ran alongside them, trying to keep up, his short legs a blur of motion.

Celina laughed, and Patrick laughed, too. The sun seemed less intense, the temperature just right. The heat wave must have broken. It was going to be a perfect day. In no time they were at the river, looking out over a wide trough of dry sand, rocks, and scattered creosote bushes.

"My dad thinks it's crazy to call this a river," Celina said. "He says it should be called a wash, or better yet, an arroyo." Her tongue fluttered over *arroyo,* shifting from English into perfect Spanish without the slightest hesitation.

Patrick looked at Celina, startled that he had forgotten about her brown skin, silky black hair, dark eyes, and her Mexican name, Celina Ortiz. He went to Dewey Elementary with lots of kids like Celina—Ramon, Leah, Carlos, Maria—but he'd never really gotten to know them outside of school. He knew how some people were about those who came from Mexico, or whose relatives had. Some people sneered and called them *wet-backs,* as if they'd all swum illegally across the Rio Grande into the country, as if they were less human than everybody else. He'd seen the looks in some people's eyes. Andy was like that on bad mood days, and wouldn't choose them for his team on the playground, even if they played well. Patrick didn't feel that way, though. Paulette said people were people; nothing else mattered. She was right. It didn't matter. Celina was Celina. Celina was his . . . yeah, his friend.

Patrick smiled at Celina, then looked back at the dry gully and shrugged. "It has water in it some of the time, like after a storm. It's a river then, right?"

Celina shook her head. "Dad says rivers have to have water in them all the time to be called rivers.

He looked it up in the dictionary." She laughed. "Mom says where else but the desert do you get to see what's underneath a river? She thinks it's neat that you can see the bottom so much of the year. She says Dad is too picky. She says that's what you get when you marry a history teacher."

Patrick stared. "Your dad teaches history?"

Celina nodded. "Yep. World history, especially about how Europeans came to North and South America, and what they did to it. And Mom teaches literature—you know, all about books. She loves poetry the best. They both teach at the university."

"You mean they're . . . "

"Professors, both of them," Celina said.

Patrick couldn't believe it. Professors? He had never met a real professor before. He'd just heard Paulette talk about them as if they were special, and had imagined that they all were old men who wore sports jackets and smoked pipes. He had always thought that they lived in those nice old houses by Hughes Park. But here was this girl telling him that the brown-skinned man and woman he'd seen dressed in blue jeans and T-shirts, sweating as they unloaded the moving van, speaking Spanish, living next door to him, were professors at the University of Arizona.

Celina pushed her hair back behind her ears.

"My dad is the first person in his family to get his doctorate. He studied in Europe. So did Mom. That's where we've been living until now—in Spain."

Living in Spain! Good grief! Patrick had seen a show on Spain once on TV. That was all the way across the Atlantic Ocean. "Spain?" he asked. "Really?"

"Yeah," Celina said with a shrug, as though having lived in Spain was no big deal. "But Dad grew up in that house beside you. When Grandma died he wanted to come back to Arizona and live in it again. He said he missed the saguaro in the backyard, buying fresh tamales by the dozen, talking to his old friends. Mom, too. She grew up just an hour away, over in Benson. They met at the university when they were eighteen. It was great when they both got jobs there. The only problem has been finding a place for all of their books." She laughed. "You should see 'em all. We've got tons. Mountains!"

Patrick tried to imagine it—the Ortiz family surrounded by books. Tons of them. Mountains! He nodded as though it all made sense, as though this story were normal, that lots of kids in the neighborhood lived that way. But it didn't really make sense. No one he had ever known had parents like that, books like that.

"Can we go down there?" Celina asked, pointing into the dry wash.

Patrick was glad for a change of subject. The desert was something he felt comfortable with. He knew it. He bet he could even teach the daughter of two professors a thing or two about it. "Sure," he said, "let's go!"

They parked their bikes behind a clump of mesquite trees, then ran down the rocky bank onto the soft, sandy bottom. "Arroyo," Celina said over and over, almost singing the word. Patrick found himself singing it, too, quietly trying to mimic the way it rolled off Celina's tongue. The sound of car traffic on the nearby bridge mixed with the singing and the sound of the cicada bugs, and faded away.

Patrick took deep breaths of air and twisted his feet in the sand with each step, bouncing from one foot to the other, a kind of dance. He sang a little louder, not afraid that Celina might hear. "Arroyo. Arroyo." Celina sang back. "Arroyo. Arroyo." She threw a stick for Pellinore to fetch, tossing it as far ahead as she could. The small dog ran after it, kicking up sand as he sprinted for his prize, and disappeared around a clump of creosote bushes. His high-pitched barking brought Celina and Patrick on the run.

Pellinore was barking at a lizard sunning itself on a large rock. "Wow!" Celina shouted. "It looks just like a dragon. Almost like the Questing Beast!" She grabbed Pellinore by the collar, holding him back. "Leave it alone, will you. Sit! Sit!"

Pellinore didn't sit. He lunged at the lizard and continued to bark.

Patrick wasn't nearly as excited as either Celina or her dog. "It's just a chuckwalla," he said calmly, feeling proud that he knew something the daughter of two professors didn't. "I've seen bunches of them."

Celina bounced up and down on her toes, still holding onto Pellinore's collar. "Really? Bunches?"

Patrick nodded. "Yeah, but I like gila monsters or just about any decent-sized snake better. When it's still this hot, they usually don't come out until night, though." It felt good to be the expert. He hoped Celina would comment on his knowledge of the desert.

She didn't, though. She was too caught up in the sight of the chuckwalla, its dry, scaly skin hanging in loose folds along its sides, its beady eyes watching them so intently.

"Can we catch it and take it back? It could be our own Questing Beast. Wouldn't that be great?

Can you catch it, Patrick? Can you? Can you?"

Patrick shrugged. "Sure," he said, "I can catch it. No problem."

But as soon as he lunged for the chuckwalla, it scurried back into a crevice and inflated itself with air. The loose folds of skin on its sides stretched tight across its body and against the rocks, wedging it in. Patrick tugged on its tail, then tugged harder.

"Not so hard!" Celina said. "Won't its tail break off?"

"That's whiptails and zebra lizards, not chuckwallas," Patrick grunted, working one hand in to grab the chuckwalla by the neck. It hissed, twisting around, and tried to bite his finger. He jerked his hand away. "They do get mad, though." He reached in again, getting hold of its neck this time, while increasing the pulling pressure on its tail. He grunted, then gave an extra tug.

The chuckwalla came loose all at once, sending Patrick staggering back. He struggled to get his balance, then held the angry, wriggling lizard up in the air. "Got it!" he yelled.

Pellinore barked.

"Yay!" Celina shouted. "Our Questing Beast. Can I hold it?"

"Sure, just be careful," Patrick said. He handed

the lizard to her. "Hold it behind the neck, just like I'm doing."

Celina reached out, eyes dancing with delight, and took the chuckwalla. "I dub you our Questing Beast!" she said with a big grin. "You're just perfect!"

Then, before Patrick could do anything to stop her, she rubbed her nose affectionately against the chuckwalla's—a *big* mistake.

Chapter 9

DON'T WORRY?

The chuckwalla bit hard into the end of Celina's nose. She fell back yelling. "Get it off! Get it off! *¡Quita me lo!*"

Pellinore snarled and barked, kicking up sand and lunging at the lizard's tail. He ended up with Celina's shirtsleeve instead. Celina rolled around in the sand. "No, Pellinore! Patrick! Patrick, get them both off!"

Patrick pushed Pellinore aside. He grabbed the chuckwalla and pulled.

Celina let out a sharp yelp. "Don't!"

Patrick let up, but the chuckwalla didn't, its jaws still clamped tight.

"Get it off! Please!" Celina pleaded, her voice

starting to quiver. "Please get it off! It's probably poisonous, or I'll bleed to death. I'm going to die!"

Pellinore started to whine. Patrick examined Celina's nose and shook his head. "Its teeth haven't even broken the skin. There's no blood. Besides, it's gila monsters that are poisonous. Chuckwallas aren't. Don't worry."

Celina glared at him. "DON'T WORRY?" She was screaming now. "THERE'S A LIZARD BIT-ING MY NOSE, STUPID!"

Patrick sat back as if pushed by the force of the word. Stupid. She knew. Her voice had sounded just like his father's. He felt a momentary rush of panic.

But just as quickly as Celina had gotten angry, she started to cry. "Do something. Please."

The quick change in Celina snapped Patrick out of his fear. He looked around, eyes darting, until he spotted a good-sized stick that had lodged up against a bush in a summer flood. He rushed over and picked it up, then ran back to Celina, who was carefully sitting up, holding the chuckwalla with one hand. Tears streaked her cheeks. Patrick grabbed the chuckwalla's tail, raised the stick, and started to give the lizard a hard whack.

Celina's scream split the air. "NO, YOU'LL KILL IT!"

Pellinore cowered. Patrick stopped in mid-swing. "I thought you wanted me to get it off."

She took a deep breath. "I do, but I don't want you to hurt it. It's our Questing Beast."

Patrick lowered the stick and sat back in the sand. "Our Questing Beast?" he said, trying to figure out just how it was that a person with a lizard biting her nose could be concerned about Questing Beasts. Maybe he hadn't heard her right. "You don't want me to hit it because you want to pretend it's a Questing Beast?"

"Yes," Celina said, "we need a Questing Beast." She looked at him, then at the lizard, which was so close it made her go cross-eyed. Patrick couldn't help but giggle.

Celina frowned. "It's not funny," she said, but then giggled, too. Pellinore barked and wagged his tail.

Patrick stifled his laughter, got up, and began to look around the wash again, calling over his shoulder. "OK, we need something to pry its jaws loose." He poked at a pile of flood debris.

Celina giggled again. "You know, I just realized that this doesn't hurt! It scared me at first, that's all. I've got a lizard biting my nose, and it really doesn't hurt!"

"Good," Patrick said, still looking, "because

there's nothing here that will work to get it off."

Celina was laughing now. "Wow! Wait until I tell my mom and dad about this!"

"You could wear it home for dinner," Patrick quipped, still looking for something to pry with. Then he had an idea. "I know!" he said, and before Celina could ask any more questions, he pulled her up and dragged her toward the bicycle—running across the arroyo with a chuckwalla attached to her nose.

By the time they got to the stoplight at the corner of Mesa Avenue and Verde Road, Celina was using her predicament like a practical joke. She waved at a woman in a red sports car, pointed to the chuckwalla, and yelled, "What will they think of next?" The woman stared with her mouth hanging open. Celina waved and pedaled off behind Patrick, then burst into laughter.

They wheeled into the parking lot of Lupita's Mexican Café. Patrick jumped off his bike and ran back to help Celina off hers. She was coasting to an awkward stop, one hand on the handlebars, the other on the chuckwalla.

"Did you see the look on that lady's face?" she wanted to know, still laughing.

Patrick smiled as he took her by the arm and led her toward the café. "Yep." He reached for the door handle. "Paulette works here. She'll help us get the chuckwalla off."

Celina jerked him back so hard, he almost fell down. "Paulette is your mom, right?"

Patrick recovered his balance and nodded. "Yeah, so what?"

A look of panic appeared in Celina's eyes. "I don't want to meet your mother for the first time with a lizard on my nose."

Patrick thought she was still joking. He laughed and waved her off. "Don't worry," he said, turning toward the restaurant door again, "she'll think it's funny, too."

"No!" Celina said, her voice rising quickly toward a screech. She lowered it, but her eyes remained fierce with emotion. "I don't want her to see me like this. I'd be too embarrassed. I'd feel stupid!"

Patrick stared. He had begun to think Celina was perfect, could do no wrong, always knew the right thing to say—to anybody. Her parents were professors. She lived in a house full of books. She spoke two languages, had lived in Spain, could read *The Sword in the Stone* as if she were born with it in her mouth. And yet, here she was . . .

"OK," Patrick said, ushering Celina to the back of the restaurant. "I'll sneak a spoon from the silverware tray." He sat her down by the service-entrance door. "Just leave it to me. *Everything* is under control."

Chapter 10

Eeeeee!

Patrick couldn't get the spoon far enough into the lizard's mouth to get any leverage. And despite everything, Celina continued to insist that he not be too forceful. "You might hurt the Questing Beast!"

A butter knife did no better. Celina wouldn't allow the use of the blade, even though Patrick kept assuring her that it wasn't sharp.

Celina nixed the fork, too, before Patrick even got out the door with it. She'd been stabbed with one once by her two-year old cousin, it seemed. "And it really hurt! The lizard doesn't."

Patrick was sure a pair of serving tongs would

do the trick. "But they don't," he said moments later through clenched teeth.

Pellinore, who had actually been very good up until then, started to whine. Patrick took a deep breath and turned to go back into the café to see what else he could find—only to look up and see Paulette standing in the doorway. "Oh, hi!" he said, moving quickly to block her view of Celina.

"What are you doing here?" Paulette said, pushing a stray lock of hair out of her face. She looked tired, but her question wasn't an irritated one. She smiled when she looked at her son. "I thought you were coming for lunch. We're just now getting the last of the breakfast mess cleaned up and—" Then she noticed Celina. She peered around Patrick to get a better look. "Who's that with you?"

"Oh, that's . . ." Patrick hesitated. "That's a friend of mine."

"A friend!" Paulette beamed. "Well, please introduce me!" And before Patrick could say anything to prepare his mother, she stepped around him and looked down at Celina.

"Eeeeee!" Paulette's scream pierced the air. She stepped back, then leaned forward, a look of pure horror on her face. "What? . . . How? . . . Oh, no!"

Celina turned beet red and looked as if she

might start crying. But within two seconds Paulette recovered from her shock and began to laugh. It wasn't a mean laugh, the kind that would make a person feel like they're being made fun of, but wonderfully high and gentle, contagious.

Patrick began to laugh almost as soon as Paulette did. Pellinore wagged his tail. Celina stared at Paulette and Patrick for a moment. Then she let out a giggle, and so it went—all three of them laughing and laughing by the service-entrance door.

However, there was *still* a certain chuckwalla attached to Celina's nose. Despite how funny it looked, and despite Celina's assurances that it really didn't hurt, everyone agreed that it had to come off.

So Paulette and Patrick set about the job together, trying other kitchen tools, giggling as they worked.

But the Questing Beast simply wouldn't let go.

Paulette went for reinforcements, then more reinforcements: Jean the waiter, Carlos the cook, Billy the dishwasher, even Lupita, the café owner. They all reacted in the same way—shock, disbelief, then laughter. They all had advice.

"Blow in its face. Somewhere I heard lizards don't like wind."

"Wait until it gets hungry. Gotta open the mouth to eat, right?"

"Tell it a joke, Carlos. It'll let go when it laughs."

"How about we call a tow truck?"

"Lupita could sing. That would scare it off."

"Hush, you two, before I roll you up in a burrito grande. Paulette, have you tried tickling this lizard under the chin?"

Lots of advice, but none of it helpful. The Questing Beast still wouldn't let go.

It was Patrick who finally came up with the solution—water.

"I don't get it," said Paulette.

Neither did anyone else.

"Huh?"

"*¿Qué, mi amigo! Agua?*"

"Water? How water?"

Patrick just smiled, went inside again, and hauled a sloshing bucket of water out. Everyone watched as he set it down in front of Celina. "Lower the lizard in," he instructed her. "All the way in, including your nose. Breathe through your mouth."

Lupita slapped Patrick on the back so hard he almost fell over. "Of course! *¡Sí!* Hold that rascal under the water until it needs air and has to let go! *¡Bueno!*" She grinned at Paulette. "You've got one smart boy here!"

Paulette beamed. "That's what I keep trying to tell him."

Patrick beamed, too. At that moment he felt smart, and brave. He motioned Celina toward the bucket. "Go on, I think this will really work."

Celina looked at the lizard, then at Patrick. "Won't it drown?"

Billy the dishwasher shook his head. "Naw. Patrick's onto something. Give it a try."

"Yeah, give it a try," everyone chorused.

Celina looked to Patrick for reassurance. He nodded. "It'll work."

"Well, OK." She took a deep breath, hesitated, took in even more air, and then carefully lowered the Questing Beast into the bucket.

Patrick and the staff at Lupita's Mexican Café gathered around Celina and the bucket like a football team in a huddle. All held their breath. All waited . . . and waited . . . and waited. Celina took a breath through her mouth. Everyone else did, too. Then the chuckwalla needed more air and let go. Celina fell back, free at last.

Everyone cheered. "Yay!" Pellinore danced around the circle, barking.

Patrick quickly fished the chuckwalla out of the bucket and held it up. "All right!" he yelled.

There was no more room on his face for a bigger grin. Everyone was clapping and slapping him on the back. Lupita, Paulette's boss, had said he was smart. He couldn't remember if he had ever felt this good in his entire life.

And to top it all off, Lupita motioned with her arms and said, "Now, come on inside. We'll take a look at this poor girl's nose to be sure it's still in one piece, and I'll treat you both to an ice-cream sundae—on the house, no charge!" She grinned. "That is, *if* you leave that rascally lizard out here in a box."

Chapter 11

Merlyn's Magic

Patrick and Celina brought the Questing Beast back to The Kingdom and gave it an honored cage to live in (an old aquarium Celina fished out of her closet).

"Let's decorate his castle," Celina suggested. The row of teeth marks across the top of her nose had already started to fade. "I'll do a coat of arms to put on the front."

Patrick made spires, which he taped to the cage corners. He drew flags that looked as though they were flapping in the wind, and stuck them in the spire tops with toothpicks.

"I wish I could draw like that," Celina said. "Could you do a picture of the Questing Beast?"

Patrick ended up doing six. The two friends worked on his cardboard castle, too, adding several turrets and a front gatehouse Celina said was called a barbican. They played chess, although it seemed that Patrick won more and more of the time. The matchup was getting uneven.

Pellinore took to sitting motionless by the Questing Beast's cage, staring intently, only to let out a whine and fidget uncontrollably if the chuckwalla so much as moved its tail. Patrick thought this was particularly funny. Some days he would spend as much time watching Pellinore as Pellinore spent watching the Questing Beast.

Celina checked out several books from the library on reptiles of the desert and read aloud the chuckwalla's habits. " 'It likes rocky areas, particularly around creosote bushes [like where we found it]. It eats palo verde leaves, and ironwood leaves, and wolfberry leaves. [What's wolfberry?] And it gets its water from its food.' Wow! It doesn't need to drink!"

But most of the time in The Kingdom was spent with Celina continuing to read from *The Sword in the Stone*. The story was getting better and better. Kay and Wart were on a quest with Robin Hood and Little John and Maid Marian to rescue Dog Boy, old man Wat, and Friar Tuck before they were enchanted by fairies. It was very exciting. Patrick and Celina couldn't wait to find out what would happen next.

Still, Patrick made Celina begin each day with those first lines that had captured him: *"There was a clearing in the forest, a wide sward of moonlit grass, and the white rays shone full upon the tree trunks on the opposite side. . . ."* Her voice danced over the words. The knight, *"standing still, and silent and unearthly,"* would appear in his mind as soon as she began. The details of that wonderful world within the book became as clear to him as as the knight's lance, *"outlined against the velvet sky."* He was there when she read. He could *feel* the story as much as hear it.

And there was that main character, Wart. Patrick grew positive that T. H. White had really been thinking of him, Patrick Lowe, when he had written about Wart. Two kids, just trying to get along in a world that wasn't as fair as it should be. Patrick and Wart. Wart and Patrick. Two kids, trying to feel OK. Patrick would beg for Celina to go on reading about Wart and complained when she had to quit and go home for dinner. It was just like the old days before he started school, when Paulette had more time and energy to read him stories, when books were something that held no demands. Celina never asked him to even touch *The Sword in the Stone,* much less read to her. With her it was fun, just simple fun.

Before long Celina had Patrick drawing all of the characters in the story. "Now listen to this description of Wart, then draw what you see in your mind."

"How about cutouts for all of them?" Patrick offered when he had finished Merlyn the wizard.

Celina grinned. "Oooo, great! You draw, and I'll cut them out."

Soon the shelves of The Kingdom were lined with the entire cast of *The Sword in the Stone.* When a particularly great scene in the book was reached—like in chapter 12, during the battle with the monstrous wyverns and griffins—Celina would stop, and the two of them would talk about what they thought might happen next, which character would do what, how they would finish that scene if they were T. H. White. Then Celina would read on. They would laugh and give each other high fives if they guessed the next turn of the story right, or marvel at T. H. White's skill if he was able to surprise them.

The Kingdom began to overflow with books. Celina brought in big volumes on the Middle Ages—"My dad let me borrow them!"—and read to Patrick about the knight's code of conduct, how they were to behave. The books called it "the code of chivalry," and listed the qualities a knight was supposed to have: truthfulness, loyalty, humility, generosity, joyful courage, and the will to fight for what was right.

Patrick loved it. Nowhere did the code say anything about reading, and the young Wart in *The Sword in the Stone* had trouble with books, too. The more Patrick learned, the more he imagined himself as part of it all. He was indeed the great White Knight—truthful, loyal, humble, generous, courageous, and always willing to fight for what was right. Celina insisted she'd be Merlyn the wizard if she were alive back then. "Even if he is a man. *I'd* be the one to work the magic."

And it seemed to Patrick that she was doing just that. Life had taken on a magical quality since Celina had come. Even school was going better. Mrs. Romero had asked him to draw a bird for the class newspaper and exclaimed over it in front of everybody when he was done. And with the weather finally cooling down, Mrs. Nagle didn't seem so irritable, even though the maintenance department still hadn't sent anyone to fix her air conditioner. She'd patted him on the back just the other day and said, "I like the way you're working so hard."

Patrick had smiled and said, "Thanks." Because he *was* working hard. For some reason, reading *The Sword in the Stone* at home with Celina made doing worksheets and drills for Mrs. Nagle seem easier.

Yeah, things were good, even Andy's moods. Maybe Andy's dad being in jail wasn't such a bad thing after all. "Pass the ball to Patrick!" he often yelled during soccer games, and picked Patrick first when choosing his team. Patrick liked that feeling and wanted everything to go on the way it was, forever. Slowly, he began to believe that it would.

Then Mrs. Romero made an announcement.

Chapter 12

Wetback

It was a Monday morning, right after lunch count, when Mrs. Romero stood in front of the class with a big smile on her face and said, "There will be a school chess club starting next week. It will meet on Tuesdays and Thursdays in this classroom during lunch recess, and I will supervise it. Chess is a wonderful game. Please join in the fun if you know how to play or want to learn."

Celina leaned across the aisle toward Patrick, eyes shining with excitement, and whispered, "You've got to join! You're the best!"

Patrick shook his head. Playing alone or with Celina was one thing. Playing at school around a bunch of kids was another. He'd never been in a chess club. He shook his head even harder. No. No way.

"But you're so good," Celina insisted. "I haven't been able to beat you for the last ten games. You could be school champion!"

Patrick acted as though he didn't hear, rummaging around in his desk. Where was that good drawing pencil?

Celina sighed, and let it go . . . until the next day.

She and Patrick were walking down the hall together when Andy and Travis Macintosh came out of the boy's bathroom. Andy had a black eye. Someone in class had whispered earlier that his dad had gotten out of jail just that morning, immediately gotten drunk, and then hit Andy. No one knew for sure, and no one was asking Andy. It had been obvious from the moment he walked in the classroom that he was in a bad mood.

"Got a boyfriend, huh, Celina?" Andy said. "I guess you love Patrick."

"Just ignore him," Patrick whispered as they walked past.

Andy turned to Travis. "But how could anybody love a wetback?"

Celina whirled around with fire in her eyes, her fists clenched. "Don't call me that! I'm just as much an American as you are!"

Patrick touched her elbow. "Forget it," he said. He kept his voice calm, even though he didn't feel that way inside. "Just ignore him." He steered Celina away.

Although he wasn't always successful at it, Patrick had had plenty of experience at practicing what he preached. He was able to ignore Andy's continued insults all day, even on the soccer field. For Celina, though, it was a constant battle, especially after Andy announced that he was signing up for the chess club himself. "I'm the best in the whole school," he sneered at her. "I guess I *have* to sign up, huh, wetback?"

Patrick acted as if he didn't hear. But Celina couldn't control herself. She sneered right back at Andy, then turned to Patrick. "You can beat him," she insisted. "I know you can. I watched him play last week during choice time. He's pretty good, but not nearly as good as you are. You could beat him with one eye closed. You know things about chess that catch me off guard all the time. You could trounce Andy and shut his big mouth forever. You'd be like the White Knight at a jousting tournament. There's no way you'd lose. You'd be school champion. You're great!"

Patrick glowed under Celina's compliments, but didn't let on. "Just ignore him," he kept repeating.

Celina couldn't, though. From then on, she reacted to everything Andy said. Any mention of
the chess club, and she turned to Patrick. "Sign
up. Beat him!" By the day before the chess club's
first meeting, she was hounding him almost constantly. "Tomorrow is the first meeting. It's in
our room. Mrs. Romero will be there. You'll do
great. You've *got* to sign up!"

She kept at it, increasing the pressure even
more after Andy called her a wetback again on
the bus. She spun great tales of victory on the
field of battle, until, after a particularly good
game that afternoon in The Kingdom, Patrick
finally gave in. "OK, OK, I'll go," he said, telling
himself he was doing this just to get Celina to
shut up, but convinced that he really could be
school champion. "I'll go. But only if you promise to go, too."

Celina burst into a big grin. "I wouldn't miss it
for all the ice cream in Arizona! It's you and me,
the White Knight and Merlyn, off to the jousting
tournament!"

The next day at school Patrick came into the
building early to tell Mrs. Romero he was going
to join the chess club. He was excited now that he
had decided to do it, and walked quickly toward
his room to deliver the good news.

Just outside of his classroom he heard his name spoken and stopped short. It was Mrs. Nagle's voice. At first, the sound of it bothered him. But then he remembered her pat on the back, and decided that she was probably telling Mrs. Romero how hard he had been working in the Resource Room. He leaned close to the doorway, careful not to be seen, smiling at the thought of spying on his teachers.

"Yes, I know Patrick is trying hard," Mrs. Nagle was saying. "It's wonderful!"

Patrick's smile grew into a big grin.

"All the more reason not to cut back on his time in the Resource Room when he's just beginning to make progress. He is *so* far behind. I don't know how he'll ever make it in middle school."

Patrick withdrew from the doorway so quickly he almost fell down. His ears rang with Mrs. Nagle's words. "He is *so* far behind. I don't know how he'll ever make it . . ." He felt stunned, as if he'd just been hit hard on the head from behind. But she had patted him on the back. He had thought he was doing so well.

Patrick turned and ran back down the hall. He had to get away, out into the fresh air of the playground.

Chapter 13

The Jousting Tournament

Despite protests, Celina would not let Patrick change his mind about joining the chess club. "A promise is a promise. You said you would. A true knight never goes back on his word. Remember the code of chivalry?"

Yeah, he remembered. Truthfulness was the first quality of a good knight.

"You'll do it, right? Say you will."

"All right," Patrick said, "I'll do it." He decided to ignore what Mrs. Nagle had said the same way he'd been ignoring Andy. He decided to ignore the uneasy feeling in his stomach, too, even though it gnawed at him right up till lunch recess when the chess club met for the first time.

There were at least twenty kids who had joined the club, mostly older, but a few second and third graders. Mrs. Romero decided she would draw names by age level to see who would play who, beginning with fifth grade.

"AND NOW!" she announced dramatically, hamming it up for all she was worth, "THE FIRST CONTESTANTS!" She held an old cowboy hat over her head. "This is my story hat," she said. "I wear it sometimes when I tell stories, because my grandpa Manuel always wore it when he told me stories as a child." She smiled. "But it's a good chess club hat, too, don't you think?"

Patrick didn't. The first two names that Mrs. Romero drew out of her "story hat" were his own and Andy Wilkinson's.

"Oh, man," Andy moaned loud enough for just about everyone but Mrs. Romero to hear. Andy looked over at Jenny Armstrong, who had come in late. "Does Patrick even know how to play?"

Patrick ignored the insult, instead imagining himself the White Knight readying to joust. Andy's words didn't change a thing, just like Mrs. Nagle's didn't. Quickly he arranged his pieces on the chessboard, blocking out the sound of other names being drawn, other boards being set up, other games beginning. He blocked out Andy's continuing moans and groans. He blocked out everything except the battle to come. His name had been drawn first. Mrs. Romero said first draw got to choose colors. No choice there. White. White was his color. He was the White Knight. And white moved first. Good. Patrick knew just the move he wanted to make: king's pawn forward two.

Andy rolled his eyes as if that were the stupidest opening move in the history of chess. He quickly answered Patrick's charge with his own king's pawn forward two also.

Patrick nodded. The kings' pawns stood face-to-face. So far, so good. Now for his king's knight—a white knight, like him. Charge! He moved it out in front of the king's bishop, threatening Andy's pawn.

Andy looked up from the board. "So, look who knows how to play chess." He surveyed his pieces. "Well, so do I." He moved his queen's knight out to protect the threatened pawn.

Charge! Patrick moved his other white knight out—bishop three. Into battle the white knights galloped side by side.

Andy didn't look up. He moved his king's bishop diagonally out in front of his queen's knight. It was a good move. Powerful pieces out as soon as possible rarely backfired.

Patrick took Andy's pawn with his king's knight.

"Ha!" Andy let out a sharp laugh. "I knew you didn't know what you were doing." With a flourish, he took Patrick's knight with his own. "I'll trade a pawn for a knight any day. Why not?" He laughed again and looked around to see if Jenny or anyone else were watching.

Patrick ignored Andy and quietly moved his queen's pawn up to the fourth square. It now threatened both Andy's knight and bishop. A fork, protected by his queen. "Sure to do damage either way you go," just like Dad had said. Charge!

Andy's grin dropped into a frown. Glaring at Patrick, he moved his queen out in front of his king. "Take one and I'll nail you."

Patrick almost let himself smile. Perfect! The enemy had made just the fateful mistake he had hoped for. He lowered his lance and galloped into the heart of the battle, moving his white knight directly between Andy's knight and bishop, threatening the most powerful piece in chess—the queen.

Patrick kept his eyes down and held his breath. Charging, charging across the sunlit meadow. After a long pause, he looked up.

Frustration showed clearly on Andy's face—his forehead furrowed, eyes glaring. Patrick was controlling the game, and now Andy had no choice.

He had to move his queen to protect it. He responded by attacking the attacker and moved his queen forward one, threatening Patrick's white knight.

Charge! Patrick quickly moved his white knight, taking Andy's bishop's pawn. "Check," he said. Not only was it check, the only way for Andy to get out of it was to lose his queen. Another fork. He had Andy. He had him!

Patrick smiled. He couldn't help it. He looked Andy right in the eye. "Check," he said again. "Your move."

The look on Andy's face was at first one of total astonishment. "That's not check," he said.

Patrick reached over and pointed to his knight, then Andy's black king. "Yeah, it is. Look."

Andy erupted, batting Patrick's hand away, bumping the chessboard. Several pieces fell onto the floor. "You cheated!"

Patrick sat back, his face growing flushed. "There wasn't anything wrong with that move!" he said. "You were in check and you know it!"

Andy grew angrier. "No, I wasn't! You cheated!"

"I did not!" Patrick shot back. He lowered his voice. "That move was OK. I know the rules!"

Andy's expression went blank, and Patrick thought he had him. But instead of slinking away, admitting defeat, Andy quickly reached over and grabbed a small paperback book from the table next to theirs. "You know so much about chess?" he growled, thrusting the book right in Patrick's face. "Here's the rule book. Read them to me, stupid!"

Patrick sat back as if pushed. He was no longer the victorious White Knight. He was Patrick Lowe, fifth-grade failure. The print on the cover of the book Andy shoved at him seemed to grow in size, reaching out for him. Then the letters blurred, and he felt a weight on his chest. The walls of the classroom began to close in. Everyone was looking at him, he knew. It became hard to breathe. He had to get out.

"Read the rules, stupid!" Andy demanded again, this time louder.

Patrick was beginning to panic. Everything looked fuzzy. Sounds echoed. He heard Celina's voice clearly, though. "Leave him alone, Andy!" He could hear Mrs. Romero's, too—calm but firm, telling Andy to back off, "Now!"

But Andy wasn't about to stop. He drowned out Celina and Mrs. Romero, yelling so that everyone in the room could hear. "How can Patrick be in the chess club? He can't even read the rules. He's too *stupid!*"

There was a great uproar. Voices full of emotion rang all around. But it was only Andy's that Patrick could hear clearly. "Stupid! Stupid!" Then his father's, at first echoing, as if from far away, then up close. "Can't get anything right! Stupid! Stupid!" Andy's and his father's words swarmed around Patrick like angry bees, stinging him, forcing him back, closing in on him, until Patrick couldn't take it anymore, broke wildly away, and ran.

Chapter 14

The Magic Book

Celina darted after Patrick. He could hear her footsteps behind him in the school hall.

"Patrick! Patrick, come back!"

He sprinted out the front door of Dewey Elementary and down the sidewalk in the blinding midday sun.

Celina followed. "Patrick, stop!"

But he didn't stop until blocks later when he plunged through the oleander bushes into The Kingdom. Celina staggered in after him and dropped to her knees, dripping with sweat, gasping for air, unable to talk.

Patrick faced her with pain and anger in his voice. "Andy's right!" he cried out. "I *am* stupid! I can't read. I'll *never* be able to read. I'll never make it in middle school. I'm too stupid. Everybody knows it! Mrs. Nagle. Mrs. Romero. Everybody probably says it behind my back. Go ahead. You say it, too. Say it to my face. Just call me stupid!"

Patrick turned away when he felt the tears well up in his eyes and his shoulders begin to shake.

Celina reached out and touched him. "No, Patrick. You're not stupid. You can read. You can!"

He spun back to face her. "You don't understand!" he yelled. "I'm not like you! I *can't!*"

But just as quickly as angry frustration filled him, it left. His voice went soft, as if someone had taken the air out of it. His next words, when they came out, had no life, only hurt and despair. "I just get all messed up. It's like I can't see regular or something. I don't know . . . I want to read, but I just can't do it the way I should. I really can't. I try. I've been working hard for Mrs. Nagle. I have. But . . ."

Patrick's voice quavered and he stopped talking, trying to get control, trying to keep the great flood of emotions he felt building up in him from spilling out like water over a dam.

"It's OK," Celina said, "don't cry."

Patrick sat up straight. "I'm not crying." He took a deep breath, then let it out forcefully. "Andy just made me mad, that's all."

Celina nodded. "If I was really Merlyn, Andy would be in big trouble right now. I'd turn him into a"—she looked around The Kingdom—"a Questing Beast. And I'd put *him* on the run from King Pellinore!" She forced a laugh. "That's what I'd do!"

Patrick looked over at the sleeping chuckwalla and tried to smile. But it was a small and fragile smile, and wouldn't stay on his lips. He sighed and looked at Celina. "If you were really Merlyn, you know what I'd get you to do?"

Celina shook her head. "No."

"I'd get you to make me a magic book, that's what."

Celina sat back, cross-legged on the dirt. She folded her hands in her lap. "How would the book be magic?"

Patrick let his gaze wander over the cutouts and the castle, coming to rest on the Questing Beast again. He tapped on the glass cage, got no response from the sleepy lizard, then looked back at Celina. "It would be magic because all you would have to do is open it and you'd know the story. There wouldn't be a tape recording, or video, or anything fancy like that inside. No one would have to read it out loud. There wouldn't even be words. You'd just open the cover, and magically you'd know the story, just like that!"

Celina burst into a wide grin. "What a great idea! Tell me the story the magic book would tell. C'mon, Patrick. Please!"

Patrick hesitated. "I don't know what it would be. Something about a White Knight, I guess. But after that . . . I don't know."

Celina scooted closer. "Yeah, a White Knight. He'd be fighting for what's right. Please tell me. It's a magic book, remember?"

Patrick took a deep breath. "Well . . ." He looked at Celina.

"Go on," she said. "Pleeeease."

Patrick nodded. It was OK. She was his friend.

"The White Knight lay near death," he began, "alone in the Dark Forest of Tuskdor."

The words seemed to come into his mind just before he needed to say them. Somehow, from somewhere deep down inside, they came. It was like a story he already knew, had already told, even though he was making it up as he went. The feeling was magical, as if Celina really were Merlyn, and she had spun another spell. She smiled, and he continued.

"He was the bravest knight to ever live, and people said he had never broken the code of chivalry . . ."

Chapter 15

Bravo!

By the time Patrick finished his story—"and the White Knight defeated the dragon and became king of all the land"—Celina was bouncing with excitement. "We've got to write it down. It's too good not to. Great stories *have* to be saved. I LOVE it!"

Patrick sat back, panic jumping into his eyes. She didn't mean that *he* should write it down, did she? No way. "I'm not going to write—"

"We could tape it," Celina quickly cut in. "All you'd have to do is tell it again, just like you did now. You wouldn't have to write a thing."

Patrick relaxed a bit, but still wasn't sure.

"We could use my dad's recorder." Celina got more excited as she talked. Her smile grew with each word, until she was almost laughing as she spoke. "It's such a great story, Patrick. Really! I love it! You can tell it again, can't you? You're so good."

"Well . . ." Patrick said, liking the feel of Celina's compliments, but at the same time not sure what it would be like to talk into a tape machine. He didn't like performances of any kind.

Celina took his *well* as a *yes.* "Great!" she said, already headed out of The Kingdom. "I wonder where Dad put the recorder . . . I haven't seen it since we moved. . . . Wow! What a story!"

Patrick couldn't help but smile at her enthusiasm. He gave in. What harm could it do? It really was a good story. He had surprised himself with it. His anger and frustration had worked to his advantage. Somehow the story had come out easier because of those feelings, as if they had formed his thoughts into words and sentences. Why not tell it again? It'd be all right. "But only if you promise that the tape will be just for us," he called after her.

"Sure, whatever!" Celina yelled back at him as she clambered over the block wall. "It's such a great story!"

*   *   *

Patrick insisted the best title was "The White Knight." "That's who the story's about."

Celina pressed for something more dramatic. "How about . . . 'Into the Shadow of Death,' or something like that?"

Patrick held firm, though. "No. I like 'The White Knight.' I can name it whatever I want. It's my story."

It *was* his story, and he proved it by telling it even better the second time. At first he was nervous, self-conscious with the tape recorder whirring on the table in front of him. But within seconds of beginning, he actually forgot the thing was there. He was swept away, slipping easily into the role of the noble White Knight in the Forest of Tuskdor. He added extra detail, described how the knight felt, put in dialogue and a lot more action.

When Patrick finished, Celina applauded and shouted, "Bravo! Bravo!" over and over again. Pellinore, who had come with Celina when she returned, barked happily.

Patrick blushed, then noticed that the tape recorder was still on. He reached for the red Off button.

Celina quickly scooped the machine up and held it out of Patrick's reach. She laughed and spoke directly into the microphone. "Yay, Patrick, the great storyteller. Bravo! Bravo!"

Patrick reached for the machine again. "Don't say that on the tape," he said. "That's embarrassing!"

But the laughter in his voice gave him away. "Bravo, Patrick!" Celina kept saying into the microphone, giggling, laughing. "He's embarrassed, but he's so great!"

Patrick faked an angry glare at her and dove for the recorder. Celina screamed and fell over backward, trying to get away. They wrestled for the machine, laughing as they rolled around in the dirt.

"Give me that!"

Pellinore barked, then licked at Celina's face.

"Yuck! I mean, Yay! Sir Patrick the Great! He's so cool!"

Patrick let Celina keep the tape player away from him, let her keep saying those wonderful things about him. The more she talked, the more distant the pain of only an hour before seemed to be. He let her go on, and on, and on. She could talk like that forever. It made him feel so good, so glad, so full of hope . . . until Paulette came home.

Chapter 16

Fever

She walked in the door three hours early, and Patrick knew right away that his mother was sick. From across the room at the kitchen table, where he sat eating leftover pizza with his left hand and drawing with his right, he could see the heat in her cheeks and the dull pain in her eyes.

Paulette didn't put up much of a fight when Patrick took over, taking her temperature—102 degrees—and giving her aspirin. She protested a little bit. "I'm all right. I'm your mother. I'm supposed to take care of you, not the other way around." But they both knew that this was the way it was sometimes in families like theirs. Kids became adults. They had to.

So Patrick ignored his mother's objections, got her into bed, and then rummaged around in the cupboards until he found a can of soup. It turned out to be cream of potato, which Paulette said was fine. Patrick heated it up on the stove, poured it into a bowl, and served it on a tray with a drawing he'd done of the Questing Beast for a place mat.

"I'm sorry I'm sick," Paulette said, reaching for Patrick's hand.

He squeezed back. "Don't worry. Just rest." She worked too hard. She was always so tired. Her whole life seemed to be spent doing things for someone else, including him. Well, now she could relax and let him do things for her. "Don't worry," Patrick said again. "Go to sleep. I'll take care of you."

The next morning, Paulette woke up feeling even worse—a pounding headache, a deep chest cough, a nose that just wouldn't stop running, and the continuing fever. She didn't object when Patrick announced he was staying home from school. "You've missed work before to take care of me. That cost money!"

Paulette blew her nose and smiled weakly. "OK. One day wouldn't hurt, I guess. I really do feel yucky, and it would be nice to talk."

But she slept all morning, even when the

phone rang and it took Patrick three rings to answer. "Just wanted to be sure everything's OK," the school secretary said. "We check on everyone who's absent. Are you all right?"

Patrick could imagine the secretary—that big lady who always wore dangly earrings—sitting behind her desk in the school office, surrounded by the smell of the copy machine. She made it sound like she really cared how he was. Did she? She was new on the job this year. He didn't even know her name.

He was almost glad to tell her that it was his mom who was sick, not him, and that he was staying home to take care of her. He wasn't skipping school, like he knew some kids did. He wasn't doing anything wrong. He was doing something right.

True, he didn't want to be at school. He'd had enough of Andy to last him a lifetime. He was sorry Andy was having such a rough time with his dad, but Patrick could feel sorrier for him from home, where Andy couldn't reach him. And if he never had to go to the Reading Resource Room again, that would be great. Forget Mrs. Nagle! She could take her worksheets, and her drills, and her lying pats on the back and . . . "My mom's pretty sick," Patrick told the secretary. "I may not be in for a couple of days, or even longer."

Celina came by after school, but had to leave almost as soon as she got there. "My dad's taking me to an archaeology lecture at the university, then out for dinner—Mexican food, of course. Some guy that has done a bunch of research on the Aztecs is talking. He's gonna show slides. Should be neat. I'll come by tomorrow. See ya."

Celina shut the front door too hard when she left. Paulette woke up. Patrick got her some water and cold medicine, and held her hand until she went back to sleep.

Minutes later another knock at the door sent him running. He ran to answer because he didn't want the knocking to wake Paulette again. He flung the door open, ready for a salesman, or some of those people who come around every now and then to tell you what religion you should believe in. He flung open the door, ready to be rude.

It was Mrs. Romero.

"Hi," she said, "I heard about your mom, and came by to see if there's anything I can do to help."

Patrick just stared. When he was little he had thought that teachers stayed at school all the time, even at night. He had been shocked when he turned the corner at the grocery store one day and saw his kindergarten teacher picking out cereal. She was shopping just like a normal person. He had turned and run. As a fifth grader he knew how silly that had been. Of course teachers bought groceries and had husbands and homes and kids and all that. But still, no teacher had ever knocked on his door before.

"Uh . . . we're OK. Mom's sleeping a lot now," he finally mumbled, wondering when Mrs. Romero would bring up the problem with Andy at the chess club. That was really why she was here, right?

Mrs. Romero smiled. "Well, good. Rest usually does the trick." She paused, then held out a cardboard box. "If you're not too busy, then, I have a favor to ask."

Patrick had been so startled by Mrs. Romero's presence that he hadn't even noticed the box. He automatically reached for it.

"These books came in the mail today," Mrs. Romero said.

Patrick jerked his hands back at the word *books*.

Mrs. Romero acted as though she didn't notice. "There's a cassette tape that goes with each book. The story is read aloud on the tape. A chime tells you when to turn the page. I haven't had a chance to go through them yet. None of the kids have either. I'm not sure if they're any good, but I was wondering if—since you're home—you'd mind listening to the tapes and following along in the books, then telling me what you think."

Patrick looked from the box, to Mrs. Romero, and back at the box. Books. The box was full of books!

"I'd appreciate your opinion, Patrick," Mrs. Romero continued, "especially on the illustrations."

Patrick looked up again. "The illustrations?"

Mrs. Romero nodded. "There are illustrations on each page. You're so good at drawing. I value your opinion, especially when it comes to art. I think of you as my class expert."

Patrick could only stare. Her expert? Really?

"I was also wondering," Mrs. Romero said, "if you would draw a knight on horseback for me, like the ones you do in your notebook, except bigger. We'll be starting a study of Europe soon, and I thought we'd begin with a bit of history. I'd like to have a knight riding above the chalkboard, for the whole class to see." She smiled. "I could bring a big piece of paper by. You're great at that sort of thing. Would you draw one?"

Draw a knight on horseback for the whole class? A big one? Give his opinion on the illustrations in the books? Patrick's mind was reeling. Class "expert"? First she shows up at the door, and then all this? No teacher had ever asked him to do this kind of stuff before.

"I know it's a lot to ask when your mother is sick," Mrs. Romero said. "But since she's sleeping so much . . . if you have time . . ." She held the box of books out toward him again. "I've got so much to do, I need help. And you're so good. I'd really appreciate it."

"OK," Patrick said. The word slipped right out of his mouth. It was as if it were coaxed to the tip of his tongue by all of the nice things Mrs. Romero kept saying, and then decided on its own to jump into the air. And his hands. They seemed to glide right out and take the box as if it were full of chocolate cake, not . . . not books!

Mrs. Romero beamed. "Wonderful! I knew I could count on you, Patrick." Then she reached out and gave him a hug. Patrick stood there helpless, with his hands full of a box of books, and got hugged before he knew what hit him.

Chapter 17

The Mural

Mrs. Romero came back an hour later with a big roll of paper under her arm. "I got halfway home and started thinking about how wonderful it would be if you would draw a whole medieval scene, not just a knight on horseback. A whole medieval scene. A mural. So I went back to school and got this for you to draw on." She held up the paper. "What do you think?"

Patrick stood in the front doorway and muttered, "Um . . . well . . ." He had put the box of books out of sight behind the green armchair in the corner as soon as Mrs. Romero had left earlier. Out of sight, out of mind, like people said. Well, almost out of mind. He'd tried to put the drawing out of mind, too. The idea of doing it for the entire class made him nervous. Why had he agreed to that? And now here was Mrs. Romero in his doorway twice in the same day, wanting him to do more, and do it even bigger.

"Imagine it!" Mrs. Romero went on. "A whole medieval scene, like you draw on your notebooks, except on this." She tapped the big roll of paper with her finger. "You've just got to see it to really appreciate what you could do. Here, let me show you. . . ."

Mrs. Romero bustled past Patrick into the living room. He suddenly found himself worrying about how the room must appear to her. Was it too messy? Did it smell like soup? Would she notice the frayed arm on the couch? Should he ask her if she wanted any tea or something? Aren't you supposed to do that kind of stuff when someone like her comes to visit?

"Could you help me with this, Patrick?" Mrs. Romero asked. She was struggling to unroll the paper on the floor. There wasn't enough room.

Patrick forgot about tea and quickly shoved the coffee table and the old rocker out of the way to make room. Still, one end of the paper had to be tucked under the couch.

"There," Mrs. Romero said when they were done. "Imagine what you could draw on that."

Patrick looked. It was the largest expanse of paper he had ever seen. He got goose bumps just looking at it, and within seconds was doing just as Mrs. Romero had suggested, imagining the things he could draw there: a jousting tournament with lots of knights and colorful tents like in *The Sword in the Stone,* a village, a castle, fields and forests. And of course there would have to be a White Knight like in his story, shield and armor brilliant in the sun, locked in battle with a fierce, winged dragon that breathed flames and struck out with horrible claws. The possibilities seemed endless. The paper called out for a mural. Suddenly, Patrick couldn't wait to get started. His eyes shone with excitement.

Mrs. Romero smiled. "Draw anything you want. Tell a story with your pictures. The class will love it!"

Patrick knew that she was going to hug him again. He could have moved away, acted as if he needed to go get his drawing pencils and markers, or invented something about soup on the stove for Paulette even though she was fast asleep again.

But he didn't try to escape. He let Mrs. Romero hug him. No one was watching. Mrs. Romero. She was like Celina, like Paulette. She had this way of making him feel good.

And that made him want to make her feel good, too. She said he was great at drawing. If that were true—and maybe it really was—then great was what this mural had to be. He wouldn't let her down. No way. He'd draw the best drawing of his entire life.

Mrs. Romero said the pictures could be a story, too. Well, he knew just the story he wanted to tell. Celina had liked it when he told it to her. He had been able to see it happening in his mind when he was telling it. Now he'd tell it again, in pictures, on that mural.

As soon as Mrs. Romero left, Patrick sat down and began to sketch, but not on the mural paper at first. He decided right away not to risk messing it up with the first tries. To begin, he drew on smaller paper, then laid each piece where he thought it might look best. The castle to one side, the jousting grounds . . . let's see . . . over in the meadow. And the great White Knight? The fight scene with the dragon had to be in the center. But he also wanted to show him in the Forest of Tuskdor, near death, like in the beginning of his story. Over to the side a little might be good, but where everyone would be sure to notice him, drawn bigger than life, like he's closer. Hmmm . . . Yeah, he'd draw the White Knight twice or more. Why not?

Patrick worked for three straight hours, stopping only to eat a peanut butter and jelly sandwich and go to the bathroom. Sometimes he drew a practice picture over five or even six times to get it just right.

Paulette continued to sleep, getting up only once for just a few minutes. Patrick began to wish she'd stay sick. Not really. He felt guilty for letting such a thought even cross his mind. But with her sick he had a good excuse for not going to school. He could draw all day long, instead.

Patrick was feeling so good he even got out the box of books and tapes from behind the green armchair. It might be nice to listen to a story while he worked.

He grabbed the first tape, the one on top, ignoring the books underneath, and put it in the cassette deck by the television. He smiled and thought of Mrs. Romero when the story began. It was about a knight defending a town from a dragon. He'd look at the pictures in the book later . . . maybe, if he had time, and give his "expert" opinion. But right now there was drawing to do. Should the White Knight be on his horse when fighting the dragon in the center of the mural? Or would it look better if . . .

On into the night Patrick worked, drawing, redrawing, arranging, rearranging, and listening to the tape, until he couldn't hold his eyes open any longer. Not wanting to leave the mural, he crawled up on the couch and fell asleep. The next morning when he woke up, the first thing he did was pick up his pencil, put on Mrs. Romero's tape, get back down on the floor, and begin to draw again.

A few minutes later, Patrick looked up to see Paulette standing by the couch in her robe. "I thought I heard your brain at work out here," she said.

Patrick had been so involved in his drawing it took him a few seconds to put two and two together. "You're feeling better," he said.

She coughed, but said, "Yep," and moved around to where she could see the mural better. "I love your picture."

Patrick sat back on his knees and surveyed his work. He had transferred several of his practice drawings onto the big paper. It *was* looking good. "Thanks," he said. "I'm doing it for Mrs. Romero. Our class is going to be studying Europe."

Paulette glanced around at the living room furniture pushed back against the walls. "Well, you'll have more room if you work on this at school."

Patrick was up off the floor in an instant. "But I need to stay here and take care of you. You look awful."

Paulette rolled her eyes. "Thanks a lot!"

"No, I didn't mean awful, just bad . . . uh, *sick* . . ." Patrick slapped himself on the forehead. "You know what I mean!"

Paulette laughed. "I know, I know." She headed for the kitchen. "But even if I do look *awful*, I can take care of myself now. I'll just rest today and go back into work tomorrow. Two days of work and two nights of classes are all I can afford to miss. We need the money. I have midterms coming up. I appreciate your concern, but I'll be fine."

Patrick followed her, continuing to protest— "You need me to fix your soup!"—until Paulette finally raised her eyebrows, looked Patrick straight in the eye, and said, "You're going back to school . . . today . . . and that is that!"

And that, in fact, *was* that.

Chapter 18

Can I Keep Them?

Mrs. Romero pushed two tables together in the back of the classroom for Patrick to lay out the mural. She let him work on it as much as he wanted. He wanted to all of the time.

Mrs. Nagle had other ideas, though. She had a new reading kit she was very excited about. "It even has a board game where you race little cars around the letter sounds," she told Patrick. She got out dice with groups of letters on them and rolled them on the board, demonstrating how to play. "OK, now your turn," she said.

Patrick rolled the dice and ended up with his little race car on a square where he was supposed to put S, Q, and U together with A, V, and E.

"Ssssss . . ." He felt pressured and couldn't remember the sound S, Q, and U make together. He'd known before. Why couldn't he recall now?

Mrs. Nagle said, "It's a nonsense word, but you can do it. Put the sounds together."

Patrick couldn't believe it. A nonsense word? Now she was going to start making him read words that didn't mean anything? He wanted to yell out, "WHY?" He didn't, though. He tried again. "Ssss . . . kkkk . . . uh . . ." But he couldn't seem to make more than noise.

Mrs. Nagle finally got frustrated and said, "Sometimes I wonder if you care at all about how hard I work to help you!" The reading time ended with Patrick doing everything he could just to keep the weight off his chest, the walls from closing in, the closet door from slamming shut in his face. He thought of the mural, imagining himself part of it, not just its creator. He rushed back to the classroom as soon as he could to resume drawing.

Everybody who saw the mural exclaimed over it—even Andy, who had apologized to Patrick as soon as he'd come back to school. Patrick knew that Mrs. Romero had ordered Andy to be nice, but still it felt good to hear him say, "You ought to be an artist when you grow up!"

Depending on the day, Andy could still get

plenty mean, though. Usually, it was Celina that he picked on, but not in class or anywhere around Mrs. Romero. There were plenty of other times and places he could dig at her with his harsh words: on the playground, in the hall, in the cafeteria, on the bus.

Patrick continued to tell Celina to ignore Andy. She would . . . every now and then. But more than likely she'd yell, "Shut up!" which only made Andy laugh and tease her more. "What's the matter, wetback?" he'd say. "Hey, wetback."

Then Mr. Gordon, the school principal, announced over the intercom that there would be a school writing contest. "I realize this is short notice," he said, explaining that stories entered had to be in by the next Monday, "but Mr. Miller, an editor at the *Daily Sun,* has agreed to be our judge, and due to certain newspaper deadlines, must have your entries by the beginning of next week."

Mr. Gordon's voice echoed over the intercom speaker in Mrs. Romero's room. "Don't let that discourage you, though. Polish up an old story, or get your creative juices going quickly on a new one. Enter the contest. The winner will have his or her story printed in the Sunday 'Accent' section, and be awarded a special plaque in front of the entire school at an assembly."

The intercom clicked off, then right back on. "Excuse me, I almost forgot," Mr. Gordon said. "Mrs. Nagle has volunteered to collect all of the contest entries. Please take them directly to her in the Reading Resource Room. Thank you."

Andy immediately started bragging about how he was going to win the writing contest. "I'm going to make up a great story," he said, turning in his seat so that Celina was sure to hear every word. "It's going to be about giant chickens that attack Tucson from outer space. Zap! Blammo! Colonel Sanders to the rescue! Fried chicken everywhere. I can do that by Monday. No sweat. I'll win for sure!"

Celina bristled like an angry dog.

Patrick leaned over and said, "Remember, ignore him."

She took a deep breath and, to Patrick's surprise, held her tongue, even later at lunch when Andy said, "Hey, Celina, you going to write a wetback story to enter in the contest?"

After school, Celina went home with Patrick, following him as he carried the mural into the living room, just as he had for the past few days. Quickly, he pushed the furniture back, got down on his knees, and started to work. He had transferred all of the practice drawings onto the big paper. They were stacked in a messy pile on the coffee table, right beside the Questing Beast, which Patrick had brought in to use as a model when drawing the dragon. Celina sat on the couch. She started reading aloud from *The Sword in the Stone*. (The battle with the horrible griffins and wyverns was over. Wart was asking Merlyn to change him into a snake.) After a few pages, though, she stopped and set the book down.

"Hey, Patrick, are you going to enter your story in the writing contest?"

"No," he said without looking up.

" 'The White Knight' is so good," Celina said, ignoring his answer. "It could win."

Patrick stopped drawing and looked up at her. "No," he said again.

Celina ignored this, too. "I know we said it was just for us, but you wouldn't have to do any of the writing." The words then came pouring out. "I could play the tape and write down everything just the way you said it. It would still be your story. You could use your practice pictures for the mural as illustrations, and make a nice cover out of construction paper. I'd do fancy lettering for the title. It'd be so good. You could—"

"No!" Patrick cut in, this time with so much force in his voice that Celina squirmed uneasily in her seat. He glared at her. Couldn't she see he was busy? He liked hearing her read *The Sword in the Stone;* the setting was so much like the mural. But he didn't like her badgering him. The writing contest? She really thought he'd want to enter? Look what had happened the last time, at the chess club. He knew she meant well, but still . . .

"Forget it," he said, "OK?"

Celina nodded. "OK." She picked up *The Sword in the Stone* again and ran her thumb over the cover. "I just couldn't help but think about how . . . you know, how it could probably beat . . ." Her voice trailed off, sounding hurt and disappointed. "Oh, well . . ."

Patrick went back to the mural. He was carefully drawing each and every stone of the castle walls, even shading two sides to make them seem three-dimensional. He wanted the whole scene to look so real, people would reach out and touch it.

Celina got down on her knees beside him. "This mural is turning out great!" she said. She ran her fingers over the drawing of the White Knight on horseback. "I think it's neat how you practice each part of it until you've got it just right."

Patrick nodded as he drew, glad she had dropped the writing-contest subject. "Thanks."

Stretching over the mural, Celina picked up the pile of practice drawings from the coffee table. "They're so good." She leafed through them, then looked at each one again more carefully. "Like illustrations in a book."

Patrick sat back from his work again. His neck was getting stiff from leaning over so much. He rubbed it and watched as Celina lay his practice drawings out in a row on the couch, then arranged them in some sort of order.

Suddenly she turned to him. "Can I keep them?"

Patrick hesitated. "Hmmm . . . I don't know . . ." He'd planned on keeping them himself; he kept everything he drew. Still, Celina liked them so much. And the real work was on the big paper, not on those little pieces. He bet Mrs. Romero would let him keep the mural after the class was finished studying Europe. He shrugged. "Well . . . I guess so. OK."

"Wow! Thanks!" Celina bubbled, and scooped the drawings up before running out the door.

Chapter 19

The Winner

On Monday, Patrick was headed down the hall to the Reading Resource Room when he saw Celina stride out of Mrs. Nagle's doorway and head in the opposite direction.

"Hey, Celina!" he called after her. But she didn't hear him.

For a moment Patrick wondered why Celina had been in the Resource Room. And was that an angry expression on her face? He didn't give either question much thought, though. There were other, more pressing things to worry about—like Mrs. Nagle.

Would she act as though there was no tension between them, like she sometimes did? Or would today be another rerun of the bad scene with the race-car game and nonsense words? Patrick almost tiptoed into the Resource Room, as if treading lightly might make things easier.

But like a bad dream come true, Mrs. Nagle did insist that Patrick play the race-car game again, until he could get all the way around the track once without a mistake. He did make it almost halfway on Tuesday, but then couldn't seem to get past three rolls without a goof. Wednesday was about the same. By Thursday, he had to force himself to sit down at the game board.

So when the intercom system clicked on, he was more than a little relieved. A break, any break, was welcome. Only ten minutes left until the end of the day. He had the rolled-up mural beside him. He would take it home and do the finishing touches tonight.

"Excuse the interruption," Mr. Gordon began. His voice was scratchy and sounded as if it were coming from very far away instead of right down the hall. "I thought you'd want to hear the news."

Mrs. Nagle let out a sigh. She turned to face the speaker. Patrick looked at the clock. Actually, there were only nine more minutes until the bell rang. Maybe Mr. Gordon had a lot to say.

"I have the results of the writing contest," Mr. Gordon went on.

Mrs. Nagle sat up straighter. "Well, good," she said to herself, picking up her clipboard and pencil.

Patrick picked up his pencil, too, and began to draw in the margin of a worksheet he was supposed to do at home. He sketched in the rough outline of a tree. He'd been working on trees for the mural lately, putting in more limbs for detail.

Mr. Gordon said, "Although many excellent stories were submitted, the winning story is so good that Mr. Miller, our judge at the *Daily Sun*, said he had no trouble picking it out."

"Cream rises to the top," Mrs. Nagle murmured to the intercom speaker on the wall.

Patrick decided to practice leaves, complete with tiny veins. Now *that* would be a nice finishing touch on the mural.

Mr. Gordon cleared his throat. "In fact, Mr. Miller likes the winning story so much that he is going to take time from his busy schedule to personally hand out the award at the assembly next Wednesday. There will be press coverage and an article with photos in addition to the winning story being printed in the Sunday 'Accent' section."

"The schools need good publicity," Mrs. Nagle said, tapping her pencil on her clipboard.

"So, keeping all of that in mind," Mr. Gordon

said, "I am pleased to announce that the winning story of the Dewey Elementary School Writing Contest is . . ."

Mrs. Nagle shifted in her chair.

" 'The White Knight.' "

Patrick felt a wave of pure terror rush up his spine. He looked up at the intercom speaker in total shock. "That's impossible."

" 'The White Knight,' " Mrs. Nagle said as she wrote it down. "Nice title, but for some reason I don't remember seeing it in the pile I turned in to Mr. Mill—"

"Written by Patrick Lowe."

Mrs. Nagle and Patrick both let out small gasps. Patrick dropped his pencil. Mrs. Nagle dropped her clipboard. It landed with a thunk, directly on her toe.

Chapter 20

Traitor!

Patrick scooped up the mural and sprinted out of the Reading Resource Room and down the hall. In seconds he was out the front door of Dewey Elementary School. He ran from the intercom. He ran from Mr. Gordon's words. He ran from Mrs. Nagle's blank stare. Down the sidewalk toward home Patrick ran, mural clamped awkwardly under his arm, feet pounding the concrete as fast as unthinkable thoughts pounded in his head. He *had* to get away. He *had* to get to The Kingdom.

But hiding there did no good. In what seemed like only seconds, Celina was rushing through the back gate and ducking into the oleander bushes.

"Patrick, you won!" she blurted. In one hand she waved a small, handmade book. The cover was red construction paper decorated with sparkle and a border of shiny ribbon. In the other hand, she held *The Sword in the Stone*. She gulped air and laughed. "You won!"

Patrick clutched the mural to him, as if gripping it tightly would keep Celina's words back.

She shook the two books in Patrick's face. "You're as good as T. H. White. You won the contest. Didn't you hear? I looked all over for you, but I couldn't find you. Mr. Gordon gave me 'The White Knight' to bring to you. Here it is. You won. I knew you would. Mrs. Nagle didn't believe the story was really yours when I took it to her on Monday. She said there was no way you could have written it. Boy, that made me mad. She wouldn't even look at it. I told her that it *was* your story; I just wrote it down. But she wouldn't listen. So I went straight to Mr. Miller at the *Daily Sun*—to his office—and showed it to him. And now you won. You beat Andy. Ha! You should have seen his face when Mr. Gordon made the announcement! You won, Patrick! 'The White Knight' will be in the *Daily Sun*, and you'll get an award, and they'll take your picture, and . . ."

On and on Celina went, building speed as she talked, her words spilling out so fast they began to run together into a jumble of excited squeaks.

Patrick sat in The Kingdom, clinging to the mural and the fantasy world he had created on it, trying with all of his might to keep everything else out. But he couldn't. Celina had done this thing to him. No matter what he said to himself, there was no denying it, no escaping that fact, no keeping her words from his ears. So he turned like a cornered animal and attacked.

"You traitor!" Patrick yelled, tossing the mural in the dirt and yanking both books out of Celina's hands.

Celina sat back, stunned.

Patrick glared. "You promised that the story would be just for us!"

"I . . . I . . ." Celina stuttered as she tried to defend herself, then finally got it out. "I thought you would want to beat Andy. I thought you wouldn't mind. The story is so good I thought—"

"Well, you thought wrong!" Patrick exploded, cutting her off. The idea of winning the contest, of a total stranger having read his story, brought the world closing in. The weight pressed on his chest. He suddenly felt hot and couldn't get enough air.

"I did it for you," Celina said, pleading with him to understand.

"You did it for *you!*" Patrick lashed back, fighting for breath, fighting to keep the closet door from slamming shut. Gathering up his anger and then unleashing it on Celina was the only way out. "*You* wanted to prove something!" he yelled. "*You* wanted to make Andy look bad. I'm stupid and can't read and write. You tricked me into taping the story so you could use it against Andy. You used my story. You used *me!*"

"No, I . . ." Celina wilted under Patrick's fire, unable to find the right words to defend herself. She fumbled around in her pants pockets, finally pulling out the cassette tape of "The White Knight." She held it out to him. "Here, take it back. I didn't . . . I didn't want to . . ."

Patrick ripped the tape from her hand. "You're a traitor!" he yelled. He took a deep breath and aimed it at Celina. "YOU LIED TO ME!" Then he tore "The White Knight" in half, right in front of her face, and threw it at her. "There! You want my story. You got it!"

"No!" Celina cried. She scooped up the pieces and held them close to her. "Patrick, stop!"

But Patrick wasn't done. He ripped *The Sword in the Stone* apart at the binding and threw it at her, too. "And take this one! I don't care how it ends. It's a stupid story, just like mine!"

One piece of the book hit Celina on the side of the face. "Ow! Patrick, don't!" She picked up *The*

Sword in the Stone, her voice growing shaky. "Please don't . . . I really thought you wouldn't mind." She started to cry. "I thought I was doing the right thing . . . It wasn't bad . . . Please, Patrick, listen to me. . . . Please . . ."

But he wouldn't. "GET OUT OF HERE!" he yelled. "AND DON'T COME BACK! THIS IS MY PLACE! KEEP AWAY!"

Celina backed out of The Kingdom on her knees, tears streaming down her cheeks, clutching the pieces of "The White Knight" and *The Sword in the Stone.* "I didn't think you would mind," she kept saying. "It wasn't wrong, what I did."

Patrick screamed after her. "YES, IT WAS, YOU TRAITOR! YES, IT WAS, YOU . . . YOU WETBACK!"

Celina let out a cry, as if wounded, and ran, dropping "The White Knight" and *The Sword in the Stone* in the dirt.

Patrick threw the tape of his story at her, wanting to hit her, wanting to hurt her. It lodged in the oleander bushes, beside a particularly large white blossom.

Chapter 21

A Closed Door

Before his anger was finally spent, Patrick destroyed the cardboard castle, tore up the cutouts, kicked over the shelves and makeshift table, and threw it all—including his chess set—into the garbage. He let the chuckwalla go, not caring that it was far from its home range, and then threw the aquarium they had used as a cage away. He dumped all the books Celina had brought in on the desert and Middle Ages over the block wall. He knocked down the plywood roof last, struggling with its awkward weight, but finally, in one great push, heaved it out of the oleander hedge to land in a cloud of dust. Then he grabbed the nearly completed mural, ripped it to shreds, and threw it into the garbage, too.

Patrick stood in his backyard dripping with sweat and panting. He nodded grimly at what used to be his secret world. Nothing remained of The Kingdom. He hoped he never saw Celina Ortiz again. He didn't care about her or her family. They were just . . . just wetbacks, like Andy said.

Celina telephoned Patrick later. "Let me explain," she began.

But as soon as he heard her voice, Patrick hung up. The ringing came again. He picked up the receiver and slammed it right back down. After that, he unplugged the phone.

Around dinnertime Celina came to the door and knocked. Patrick knew it was her. He could tell by the way she banged with her palm flat instead of a fist like most people. But he stayed in the kitchen eating the leftover burritos Paulette had brought home from Lupita's the day before.

"Patrick, please answer the door," Celina called out. Then she switched tactics. "Paulette. Paulette, it's me, Celina. Can I talk to you for a minute?"

Patrick kept on eating. Celina could yell all she

wanted. Paulette wasn't home. She was working the breakfast, lunch, and dinner shifts for a few days. She was trying to make up for the salary she lost when she was sick, plus save a little for next semester's tuition at the community college. And after work she was going from the restaurant straight to class. One of her professors had offered to help her prepare for her midterm exam if she could put in some extra time. Patrick had only seen her for a few minutes over a bowl of cereal that morning. "I'm sorry," she had said at least a dozen times, "this won't be for long." That morning he had been sorry, too. Now he was glad she was gone. He didn't want Celina talking to her. He took another bite of burrito and nodded grimly at the front door.

The next morning, Friday, Patrick said good-bye to Paulette, waited until eight o'clock, then plugged the phone in just long enough to call the secretary at Dewey Elementary and tell her that he had caught whatever it was his mom had had. "Some kind of bad flu," he said, coughing into the phone. "I'll probably be out for at least a week."

Celina came back that afternoon. Patrick ignored her continued knocking again. She could knock forever for all he cared. Wear her hand out. He wasn't going to answer, even when she said, "I know you're in there and you're not really sick." Maybe he'd never go back to school. Maybe he'd just stay inside on the couch for the rest of his life. *That* would show her.

But a half hour later it wasn't Celina's knock or Celina's voice that Patrick heard on the other side of the front door.

"Patrick? Patrick?"

Mrs. Romero! Patrick jumped up from the couch and started to run in the opposite direction. Celina had gone back to school and told on him. She'd told Mrs. Romero that he really wasn't sick.

"It's me, Maggie Romero."

Patrick stopped in the middle of the living room floor. Maggie? He had never heard a teacher use her first name with kids before. Maggie? He liked the sound of it, the way she said it. He also liked the way it made him feel. It seemed special that she had used her first name with him. It was like she really knew him, and that he really knew her.

Still, he'd skipped school. He wasn't sick. Maggie or not, she would know that with one look. Maggie or not, she was still his teacher. Maggie or not, he was in big trouble. He should go on and run for it.

"Please open the door. I want to talk to you about something."

Or maybe it was the mural she was there about. Why had he torn that thing up? It was for the whole class, not just for Celina. But Celina had probably seen him rip it to shreds and throw it in the trash. She'd probably told Mrs. Romero *everything*. Patrick began to panic. Skipping school. Tearing up the mural. Mrs. Romero was probably really angry and would—

"I've been worrying about you, Patrick."

She didn't sound really angry, though.

"Are you all right?"

She sounded concerned.

"We missed you at school today."

Missed him?

"*I* especially missed you."

Patrick turned and faced the front door. Really? Really, Mrs. Romero?

"Please, Patrick, let's talk," she said.

Patrick took a deep breath, walked to the door, and opened it.

Chapter 22

The Bet

Mrs. Romero was in the living room and giving Patrick a big hug before the door was halfway open. "Patrick!" she beamed. "It's good to see you."

He waited for her smile to vanish when she realized he wasn't really sick. He waited for her to say, "But what's this I hear about you tearing up the mural?"

Mrs. Romero just kept on smiling at him, though. "You are an important member of our classroom," she said. "I really did miss you today."

Patrick blushed and looked away.

"I read your story, by the way," she continued.

"It's wonderful! I knew you had it in you. Congratulations!"

Two emotions—fear and pride—surfaced in Patrick at exactly the same instant.

"Celina showed it to me," Mrs. Romero said.

Then another emotion rose in him—anger. Nothing more than the mention of Celina's name . . .

"But just in case you're worried about it," Mrs. Romero said, "I want you to know that you don't have to get up in front of everybody at the assembly on Wednesday. It's your story. You won. But you don't have to get up on that stage if you really don't want to."

Patrick turned and eyed Mrs. Romero closely. Did she know Celina had entered his story in the writing contest without telling him? Or did she just know how much he hated being the center of attention. Either way, she was on the right track. The thought of standing up in front of the whole school to receive an award terrified him.

"It's your story," she said again. "You do what you want."

"Really?" he said.

Mrs. Romero didn't hesitate with her answer. "Absolutely."

Patrick then knew what he really wanted to do. "Can I take it out of the contest?"

Surprise showed clearly on Mrs. Romero's face. "But, Patrick, you won."

He nodded. "There was a second-place story, wasn't there?"

"Well . . . yes," Mrs. Romero said. "Andy Wilkinson's story was judged second place."

"So make Andy's first place," Patrick said quickly, getting the words out before they got caught in his throat. Andy getting the award would serve Celina right! "And the third-place story would then be in second place," he added, almost cheerfully now, "and on and on like that."

"But, Patrick," Mrs. Romero said, "I don't think—"

"That's what I want to do," Patrick cut in. He didn't mean to be rude, but she had said he could do what he wanted. Well, this was it: Pretend there was no story, never had been. No award either. Let Andy have it. Go on back to school. (Paulette wouldn't let him stay home anyway. He knew that. He might as well go back on his own.) Mind his own business and make sure everyone— especially Andy and Celina—minded theirs. Act like none of this had ever happened. That was what he wanted to do. He'd made up his mind.

Mrs. Romero didn't seem nearly as convinced. "Why don't you give it some thought over the weekend," she said, "and tell me what you've decided on Monday morning? Don't decide right now. You won. You deserve that award. Think about it, OK?"

Patrick started to say no, but hesitated, then nodded instead. This was Mrs. Romero. She was nice. "OK," he said, just to make her happy.

But deep inside he knew he had already thought about it all he needed.

Saturday morning at breakfast, Paulette said, "Mrs. Romero had dinner at the café last night."

Patrick tried to act like this was nothing to worry about. "Good," he said, and kept on eating his cereal.

"She told me all about the writing contest," Paulette added.

Patrick got up from his stool and went to the refrigerator, where he pretended to look for orange juice he knew wasn't there. He'd drained the bottle two days ago.

"I think you ought to accept the award," Paulette said. "I'm so proud of you. Aren't you proud of yourself?"

Patrick kept his head in the refrigerator.

"Don't you want people to—"

"Look, it's my story!" Patrick blurted out, turning back toward her. His voice came out with more force than he meant it to. He wasn't mad at Paulette. Still, it *was* his story. No one else should have anything to say about it. "Mrs. Romero told me I could do what I want," he said in softer tones. "What I want is to forget about it."

Paulette sighed and said, "All right." But she couldn't seem to keep from bringing the story up whenever she was home during the weekend, wanting to read it, wanting to hear all about it. "What was the title again? 'The White Knight'? I like that."

Patrick had made up his mind, though. Politely, he just changed the subject. He wouldn't give an inch.

On Monday morning Andy Wilkinson was waiting for him on the soccer field.

"How could you have written the best story in the whole school?" Andy demanded, striding toward him.

Patrick did a quick right-hand turn and walked toward the school door. Pretend it never happened, he told himself. Ignore Andy like you've done before. He's mad because he came in second in the writing contest. Bad mood day. Just ignore it. He'll be happy enough when he learns he's been bumped up to first place. Then maybe life can get back to normal.

But Andy kept on, this time loud enough to turn heads. "Who really wrote that story, huh? Your wetback girlfriend?"

Patrick stopped and whirled around, anger shooting up in him like a geyser. "She's *not* my girlfriend," he said between clenched teeth, "and *I* wrote the story."

Andy's laugh was harsh. "That's not your story. You couldn't have written it. Liar. Cheater."

Andy's words rang in Patrick's ears. Quickly he drew a mental picture of himself as the White Knight with shield and lance, riding across the sunlit meadow away from all of this. He strained to keep the image in his mind. He had drawn it so many times, lived it in his imagination for so many more. He could keep it up now, couldn't he?

He couldn't. Exiling Celina from The Kingdom and tearing it all down had somehow torn down the world inside his head, too. He couldn't shut all else out. Things began to close in on him, especially Andy's voice.

"You couldn't have written that story. You're too stupid."

Patrick began to panic. Stupid . . . Stupid . . .

Stupid. The word echoed, and with that echo the weight bore down on his chest, the air pressed in like walls, the closet door began to slam shut.

"You can't even read!"

He couldn't get enough air. In desperation, Patrick fought back. "I CAN TOO READ!" he shouted.

With that Patrick's fear cleared just enough for him to see Andy step up very close, only inches from his face. "Oh, yeah?" Andy said, making sure everyone—and there were lots of kids now who had stopped playing to watch—making sure everyone could hear. "Well, then, prove it. Read from your story at the assembly on Wednesday, in front of the whole school. Let's hear how great you are. I bet you can't."

Patrick glared back. Out of the corner of his eye, he saw Celina step toward him. She was about to butt in, he could tell. She probably wanted to say she had done the right thing again, make excuses, tell more lies. He quickly glanced over at her, letting his fierce stare speak for itself. Keep out of my life, traitor!

Celina stopped. Patrick looked back at Andy. He'd show him. He'd show Celina. He'd show everyone. The White Knight would rise to the Black Knight's challenge and fight for what was right. He would defend the code of chivalry from the forces of evil. And he'd do it alone, without anybody's help.

"OK, I'll read," Patrick said. The force of his anger and determination pushed the words out of his mouth. "I'll read my story in front of *everybody!*"

Chapter 23

Not at Home

Mr. Gordon broke into a big grin when Patrick came up to him in the hall and told him he wanted to read his story aloud at the awards assembly. "Sure!" he said. He patted Patrick on the back. "We hadn't planned on it, but of course, you won first place. It would be great to hear the winning author read his own story."

Patrick turned and looked defiantly at Andy, who had followed him from the playground to be sure he really asked.

So there!

As soon as Patrick got off the school bus that afternoon, he went straight to the garage. What had been The Kingdom was now just dirt and oleander bushes. But beside the piece of old plywood that had served as The Kingdom's roof were the two halves of "The White Knight," lying in the dust where Celina had dropped them. Patrick picked them up, thankful that he had only torn his story into two pieces instead of confetti, thankful that the monsoon season was over and it hadn't rained since. He brushed the halves off and took them inside, where he taped them back together.

Patrick sat at the desk in his room. With his jaw set tight and his shoulder muscles rigid, he opened "The White Knight" and forced himself to look his own words right in the eye.

For hours he labored over his story. Again and again he looked at the neatly printed words, straining to make sense of each little letter and sound. He used his anger to keep himself going. "C'mon!" he said to himself through clinched teeth whenever he felt like giving up. "This is your story."

But by ten o'clock that night Patrick still didn't seem to be any closer to reading "The White Knight" the way he knew he would need to on Wednesday. The fact that he had told it into a tape player didn't help him figure out each printed word. He knew how the story began, its middle, the end, and a lot of the details. But now he had to actually read it. He'd said he would, in front of everybody. To read, he had to know each word, each series of letters hooked together on the page. And each word had to go with the next and the next to make sentences, then paragraphs. Sure, some of the words he could remember. But many he had to force himself to slowly, painfully sound out. By the time he made it through those, what he had was a jumble in his mind that made no sense. Nonsense words again. He would get so intent on each individual sound, he'd completely miss the meaning.

Patrick kept on, though, turning out the light only when he heard Paulette come in from class. He jumped quickly into bed and pretended to be asleep. It felt weird, dishonest. But he didn't have enough energy or time to discuss the whole thing with Paulette right then. After he was sure she was asleep, he sat up, turned on his flashlight, and worked some more. He had to find a way to read . . . *any* way that would work.

Mrs. Nagle was more than a little surprised when Patrick showed up at the Reading Resource Room Tuesday morning before school. "You want *what?*" she said, disbelief ringing clearly in her voice.

"Worksheets," Patrick repeated. He'd made up his mind. He'd do whatever a good knight had to, even dreaded worksheets. "I'm studying extra."

Mrs. Nagle cocked her head and studied Patrick for a moment. "Mr. Gordon told me about you wanting to read your story at the assembly tomorrow."

"Do you have some extras I can take with me?" Patrick asked.

She nodded. "Yes, I do. But—"

"Thanks," Patrick interrupted, holding out his hand.

Mrs. Nagle let out a sigh. "All right, if that's what you want." She turned and quickly gathered a handful of worksheets. "Maybe there is a silver lining in this cloud," she mumbled as she gave them to Patrick. "You never know . . . You never really know . . . Here you are. . . . Come back if you need help."

Patrick worked feverishly in class that morning, driving himself, going over and over the worksheets, trying to figure out how they fit into the puzzle of words. He made a point not to look at anyone, especially Celina or Andy, or Mrs. Romero. He didn't even glance back at the new piece of mural paper Mrs. Romero had quietly set out for him on the back tables. He appreciated it, but right now he had too much to do. The mural and everything else could wait.

But when Patrick stayed at his desk, hunched over the worksheets after the rest of the class went out for recess, Mrs. Romero came and sat down right in front of him. He couldn't ignore that.

"Hi," he said, looking up.

She smiled, but then quickly turned serious. "I heard about the assembly. Mr. Gordon told me."

Patrick acted as if there were nothing unusual about volunteering to read in front of over five hundred people. But he didn't look Mrs. Romero in the eye when he said, "Yeah, no big deal." Head back down, he returned to his worksheets.

"You don't have to prove anything to anyone," Mrs. Romero said gently.

Patrick shrugged and kept on working.

"This is your story, not a string of letters and sounds. Worksheets won't help."

Patrick said nothing.

Mrs. Romero let out a sigh, and for a moment Patrick thought that it sounded a lot like one of Mrs. Nagle's sighs. "I would like to help," she offered. She reached out and put her hand on his. "If you want me to."

For an instant Patrick was tempted. Mrs. Romero was a good teacher. She was the only teacher who had ever made him feel good about himself. And she never pressured him or made him feel stupid. She had put the new mural paper on the back tables without one question as to what happened to the first. She hadn't mentioned that the class had already started their study of Europe and that the mural was past due. She'd just provided more paper. She hadn't given up on him as her "expert" artist.

She hadn't given up on him being able to read either. "You can do it," she often said. Maybe he could . . . maybe if she helped . . .

No. He was the White Knight. He had to fight alone to defend his honor and the code of chivalry. He had to fight alone to read. He could get it right. He'd prove to Andy and Celina and Mrs. Nagle and everybody that he wasn't stupid!

"Thanks," he said, "but I don't need any help."

Patrick doubled the amount of time and energy he put into the battle with his own story. He pushed himself like he never had before, ignoring everything but his goal, ignoring the ever-present threat of the closet door slamming shut in his face, trapping him in stifling darkness.

But by Tuesday night, the night before the assembly, Patrick still couldn't read "The White Knight." He sat alone in his bedroom and knew he had failed. Letters and sounds were echoing constantly in his brain. He was confused, frustrated, and utterly exhausted. He couldn't get it. He simply couldn't make it all come together and work. He had fought and fought, but there was no victory in sight.

Patrick fell back on his bed, tears welling up in his eyes. A weight pressed down on his chest. It became hard to breathe. The walls began to close in. The closet door came slamming shut.

"NO!" Patrick sat up with what felt like his last bit of strength. He ran out of his bedroom. "Paulette!" he called out, knowing she was working late and then studying, too. He needed her. He needed his mother. "MOM!" He wanted her to scoop him up in her arms and make everything else go away, just like when he was little. He rushed to the kitchen. "MOM!"

The kitchen was empty. The cupboard-lined walls began to move in from the sides. Patrick turned and ran for the phone. He began dialing Celina's number. If she would just admit that she was wrong, he'd forgive her and she could help him. He needed her help. He hated to admit it, but he did. She'd know what to do. If he could just hear her voice again, that would be good. If he could just hear her read those first lines she had read from *The Sword in the Stone*. How did they go? Something about, *"There was a forest in the . . ."* Or . . . no . . . What was it? He'd forgotten! He'd forgotten those lines he had heard so many times. And how did the story end? Suddenly, knowing how the story ended seemed very important.

Patrick finished dialing Celina's number in a near panic. He *had* to talk to her. He *had* to talk to her *now*.

But there was no one there, only an answering machine with Celina's dad saying they couldn't come to the phone right now and to leave a message after the tone.

Patrick slammed down the receiver. Scooping up "The White Knight," he ran out of his house. In seconds he was on Celina's porch, pounding on her door.

But there were no lights on, and no matter how hard he pounded, Celina didn't answer. She wasn't home. Only Pellinore was there, barking on the other side of the door.

Patrick sprinted back to his house. He slammed the door shut and threw his story across the living room. It hit the shelves, knocking some of Paulette's cassette tapes onto the floor.

Paulette. Where was his mother when he needed her? Patrick ran over and kicked at her tapes. Where was she? She was just like Celina—

not at home. The whole world was not at home! He kicked at the tapes again, sending one of them across the room and under the couch, then turned and stomped on another, cracking the plastic case.

It felt good to take out his anger on something. Patrick raised his foot, set on breaking every one of the tape cases. It would serve Paulette right for not being home when he needed her. She deserved to lose her music. She deserved to never dance again.

Patrick stopped. It had been such a long time since Paulette had danced across the living room floor, arms outstretched, head thrown back like a ballerina. It seemed like forever, since before Dad had left. But now the thought of her doing it was with him, and it wouldn't leave. The image was so real in his mind he could almost see her, smiling and dancing as clearly as if she were actually there.

A heavy blanket of guilt fell on Patrick, pushing him to his knees. He picked up all the cassettes. He switched Paulette's cracked case with one of his own. (He didn't listen to the tape in it anymore anyway.) He neatly arranged the tapes back on the shelf, making sure each and every one was lined up in a perfect row. Then he decided to straighten up the rest of the shelves, too.

That would be a nice thing for Paulette to come home to. It was the least he could do.

It was on the bottom shelf that Patrick found the tape Mrs. Romero had brought to him when Paulette was sick. It was the one he had listened to so many times when he was working on the mural—the story of the knight who defeated the evil dragon. Turning it over in his hand, he could imagine the narrator's voice telling the tale. Even though he hadn't listened to it for a while, he could hear each and every word as if it were being spoken now.

Patrick burst into a sudden grin. In seconds he was out the back door, flashlight in hand, searching through the oleander bushes.

It took him only seconds to find the tape of "The White Knight." It was still lodged in the bushes by that particularly large white blossom. He grabbed it and ran back toward the house, leaping up the steps in excitement.

Sure! He'd just listen to it over and over, like he had Mrs. Romero's tape. He'd memorize his own story—every single word of it. Then he could act as if he were reading it at the assembly tomorrow. He hit himself playfully on the forehead with his hand. Why hadn't he thought of this before? He'd been so caught up in trying to read each word, each little sound . . .

Patrick darted into the living room, straight to the tape player. He inserted "The White Knight" tape, punched the green button, adjusted the volume, and then sat down on the couch. His own voice came loud and clear from the tape player speakers.

"The White Knight lay near death, alone in the Dark Forest of Tuskdor . . ."

Chapter 24

The Dark Forest of Tuskdor

Wednesday morning the students of Dewey Elementary School filed down the hall toward the gym—all classes, every single kid. It was time to go to the awards assembly for the writing contest.

Patrick walked with his class, eyes straight ahead, not talking. He didn't want to take his mind off his story. He knew it by heart. Forward. Backward. He could probably say it upside down if he had to. He could stand up in front of all of those kids and teachers and that editor, Mr. What's-His-Name, and tell his story, no problem. He could look down at his paper and act as though he were reading. He could do it just as he had in front of the mirror last night—over and over again. No one would know he wasn't really reading. He could do it, and show Andy and Celina and Mrs. Nagle. He'd be the White Knight riding victorious, just like in his story. They'd see!

But then Celina suddenly dropped back in line and was beside him. She started talking fast.

"I know you're going to tell me to get away, but before you do I just want you to know that I've been thinking a *lot* about everything, and I'm really sorry. You were right. I shouldn't have entered your story in the contest without your knowing. Being angry at Andy, wanting to get back at him, is no excuse. You were right. I was wrong. I'm sorry. Really."

Patrick kept walking down the hall, eyes straight ahead, concentrating on his story.

Celina stayed right beside him. "But I'm not sorry I love your story. I'm not sorry I thought it would win. Because it did. You're not stupid like Andy said, or Mrs. Nagle thinks, or you said yourself that day. 'Just call me stupid,' you said. Well, no way! You're not stupid. You're smart. You can draw and play chess and write great stories. You're so good you could be a professional writer someday. You're brave and truthful and everything a knight should be. You're the White Knight, Patrick. I believe in you. I'm sorry I wasn't a good friend before, but I'll be one now. No matter what happens, I won't stop."

Patrick continued walking down the hall, expression unchanged. But Celina's words reached deep inside him, and he could feel his anger at her softening. A part of him began wanting to thank her for apologizing, tell her how afraid he was, ask her to stand up there beside him on the stage and read his story for him.

The rest of Patrick was still hurt and angry, though, and determined to show everyone—*especially* Celina—that he could do it alone, that he didn't need help, that he could read. That other part wanted to lash out, call her names again, even really hit her this time. That other part of Patrick was a balled fist, ready to take a swing.

Patrick walked and stared, torn, not knowing what to do or say, when just as suddenly as Celina had appeared, Principal Gordon and the newspaper editor were by his side, too.

"Patrick, this is Mr. Miller from the *Daily Sun,*" Mr. Gordon said, sweeping Patrick out of line and over to a tall man with a red tie. "He'll be presenting the award."

Before Patrick could begin to look up into Mr. Miller's face, Mr. Miller was extending a big hand. Words came with the handshake. "Great story, Patrick . . . love it . . . real talent . . . writer someday . . ."

Patrick gave a shy nod, and forced a quiet *thanks* toward his lips. But it didn't have time to get there. Mr. Gordon and Mr. Miller quickly ushered him away from Celina and into the gym, through the noisy crowd of kids getting seated, up the squeaky wooden stage stairs to a chair of honor. And before Patrick could do more than gawk at how big the gym seemed today and how full of faces it looked from way up there, Mr. Gordon was at the podium, talking into a microphone, his voice filling the room, echoing. Then Mr. Miller got up and talked into the microphone, too, his voice echoing, filling the room.

Patrick heard his name being called, and Mr. Gordon was prodding him out of his chair and up to Mr. Miller. A piece of paper and another handshake, there in front of everyone. Applause. Loud noise. Echoes. Big room. Big crowd. Big podium. Big microphone.

"Patrick Lowe," Mr. Miller said, "our first-place winner."

Suddenly everything was very quiet as Patrick found himself opening the cover of his story. He looked down at the first page—so carefully lettered by Celina—but didn't focus. Just as he had practiced, Patrick looked . . . but didn't focus. That was the key: Pretend to look at the words. Pretend to read.

Patrick glanced up from his book to the gym full of faces. He could act as though he were seeing them, too, instead of only the back wall. He forced a smile onto his face, then returned his unfocused gaze to his story. He was the White Knight. He could do it. He gathered in a breath and began.

"The White Kn— KNIGHT." His voice caught in his throat, then came out louder than he intended. It echoed as it filled the gym. Patrick stopped for a moment, startled by the large sound of himself through the microphone and speakers, but then quickly began again. He had to keep going. Pretend to look at the words. Pretend to read. Pretend to look up occasionally at the gym full of faces. Don't stop. Whatever you do, don't stop. Keep the fear away. Keep the weight and the walls back, the closet door open. Don't stop.

"The White Knight lay near death, alone in the Dark Forest of Tuskdor. He was the bravest knight to ever live, and had never broken the code of chivalry."

The words came out of Patrick's mouth, into the microphone, through the speakers and out into the gym—echoing, filling the room: ". . . bravest knight . . . never broken the code of chivalry . . . bravest . . . never broken . . . valiant . . . code of chivalry . . . chivalry . . . chivalry . . ."

The echo stopped. Patrick stopped, too. Even though he knew he must not, he did. It wasn't the echo or the gym full of people that stopped him. It wasn't the sight of the words on paper either. He had only pretended to read. No. It was the meaning of the words Patrick had spoken that stopped him cold on the stage. His words. They sounded false. How could he tell his story—pretending to be the lone White Knight, pretending to be honorable—at the same time he was lying through his teeth? What he was saying, and what he was doing, were two completely different things.

Patrick looked out over the microphone at the faces in the audience, not the back wall. They knew he was a liar. They had to. He looked back at his story. But maybe he could stop the lie. Maybe if he concentrated, really focused on the words and concentrated, he could actually read. . . .

The walls rushed in on Patrick as soon as he focused on the first page of his story. A suffocating weight pressed in, too. He couldn't breathe. His body and mind went numb. His ears began to ring. He quickly looked away, back to the audience.

People were starting to turn to each other, exchanging looks, then turning back to him. Someone giggled. Behind him Patrick heard Mr. Gordon whisper something to Mr. Miller. Each and every one of them knew.

Patrick panicked, seized by the overwhelming need to get away. He *had* to get away. Everything went blurry—words, faces, the deafening roar of everyone staring.

Voices began to echo in Patrick's head—first his father's, then Andy Wilkinson's. "Stupid!" He could imagine all the audience quickly joining in. "Stupid! Liar! STUPID LIAR!"

Patrick wanted to scream, "NO!" But he couldn't get a breath. He had to get away. He had to run!

Forcing his eyes to focus again, Patrick frantically searched the gym for the nearest exit. The room was beginning to tilt and swirl, still closing in from all sides. Everything was going dark. He was sure he would die if he didn't get away! Across the sea of faces his vision sped, searching for a way out.

Then Celina stood up. She stood up in the middle of the seated audience, and she smiled.

A light in the rapidly approaching darkness.

Patrick latched onto Celina's eyes and her smile with all of his might. It took every single ounce of his concentration, but he latched on. And when he did, he could hear her words in his head as clearly as if she were saying them through the microphone and the speakers on the wall. *You're brave and truthful and everything a knight should be. You're the White Knight, Patrick. I believe in you . . . I believe in you . . . I believe in you. . . .*

Echoing, echoing. Her words echoing in his head. Celina nodded her encouragement, her smile growing warmer.

I believe in you.

Another face came into focus. Mrs. Romero's. She was smiling her encouragement, too.

I believe in you.

Then Patrick saw a movement at the back of the gym, and there was Paulette. Paulette! Mom! She had given up work and study to come and hear him. She was smiling, too.

I believe in you.

Slowly, the tilting, swirling of the gym stopped. Patrick looked around. The double exit doors at the foot of the stage steps were within twenty feet. Beyond them was the playground, the sidewalk, a way out. In a matter of seconds he could be gone.

Patrick looked back at Celina, Mrs. Romero, Paulette.

We believe in you.

It was true. They *did* believe in him.

The gym walls receded, and with them the dark, suffocating weight. The closet door was open. He could breathe again. And he could see clearly.

We believe in you.

He could see that there was another way out besides the gym doors. It was the way a true knight—the bravest to ever live, who had never broken the code of chivalry—it was the way the White Knight would choose.

Patrick put down his story and forced himself to look directly at the faces in the crowded gym again, even at Mrs. Nagle, then Andy Wilkinson.

He took a deep breath. "I can't read so great," he said. "But this is the story I made up, and I can tell it pretty well."

He found Celina, then Mrs. Romero and Paulette. They all continued to smile their encouragement.

Patrick smiled back.

"I can tell it pretty well," he said again.

And with a clear voice and shining eyes, he did just that: "The White Knight lay near death, alone in the Dark Forest of Tuskdor . . ."

Chapter 25

A Clearing in the Forest

The next day, when Patrick went down the hall to the Reading Resource Room, Mrs. Nagle said, "I guess we could give this classroom thing a try . . . for a while, anyway."

Patrick stood and looked at her with his mouth hanging open. Sure, he'd seen her stand for the big ovation after he had finished telling "The White Knight." She had even privately complimented him later, too. "It was good, Patrick, very good," she had said. "Well, I *loved* it." And yes, she had then added, "Perhaps I've misjudged a few things." But still, just what did she mean, *give this classroom thing a try?*

"Work on your reading there," Mrs. Nagle

said. "With Mrs. Romero. For a while. Then we'll see."

Although Patrick understood what Mrs. Nagle was saying, the reality of what it meant still didn't sink in. He started to ask when, why, how come? But Mrs. Nagle shooed him away with what he thought might be a small smile. "Go on now. Back to your classroom for reading."

Which should have made Patrick happy. After all, there had been lots of compliments to go along with the standing ovation— "Great story, Patrick! Yeah!" And then there was the double layer chocolate cake Mrs. Romero and Paulette had made for him last night—the two of them in the kitchen, laughing and talking as they worked. He and Celina were friends again, too. She had accepted his apology for calling her names with a big smile. "Hey, no problem!" she had said. "I know you were just upset." And now, to top everything off, there was this news from Mrs. Nagle. He could go back to Mrs. Romero's room for reading. No more race-car games, nonsense words, and worksheets. What else could he ask for? He should feel better than happy. He should be dancing down the hall with a grin on his face a mile wide.

But Patrick didn't feel like dancing. He walked slowly back to his classroom and stood silently in the doorway, thinking that maybe this wasn't such a great idea.

What if "The White Knight" were just some weird kind of an accident? What if the next time he tried to come up with something it was stupid? Or worse yet, what if he couldn't come up with anything at all?

And what if the weight and the walls came pressing back in on him, the closet door slamming shut and trapping him with no air to breathe? He'd done OK telling his story in front of the gym full of people. Something had come over him. He'd felt . . . suddenly strong, sure of himself. He'd believed he could do it, and he had.

But what if that were just a fluke, and he was his same old self again today? Telling a story was different from reading one, and everyone in Mrs. Romero's class was reading—at their desks, on the old couch Mrs. Romero had dragged in, on the carpet, sprawled on the big pillows in the class library corner. Everyone was reading, and if he was to be there and not at Mrs. Nagle's, he would have to do the same.

Sure, Mrs. Romero kept on saying he could do it. But Andy said that he had lost the bet, that he didn't read . . . that he *couldn't*. "You admitted it in front of everybody." Then Andy had whis-

pered that word under his breath. "Stupid."
What if Andy was right?

Patrick stood in the doorway, thinking about
what would happen if he just went back to Mrs.
Nagle's instead of going in. He had hated it there,
but at least he'd always known what to expect.
What if he turned and left? Maybe he should . . .

But Mrs. Romero looked up and saw him. And
without a word she was there at his side, gently
ushering him to the big stuffed "Reader's Chair"
by the couch.

Patrick hesitated. He had never been in the
Reader's Chair before.

"Have a seat," Mrs. Romero finally whispered.
"It's the best one in the house."

Patrick sat, and was surprised to feel how
smooth the cushions were, how soft and silky to
the touch.

Then Mrs. Romero was handing him a
book—a big book. "Celina said you might want to
start with this one." She smiled at him. "It's yours.
A gift from your admirers. Relax. Have fun."
And she was gone.

Patrick watched Mrs. Romero go, then, not
wanting to look around the room, not wanting to
see the kids in the class stealing glances in his
direction, not knowing what else to do, he looked
down at the book Mrs. Romero had given him.

The Sword in the Stone. The picture on the front of Wart pulling at a sword stuck in a big, anvil-like rock told it all. The title printed there wasn't necessary. In his hand lay a brand-new hardback copy of the book Celina had loved, and he had once loved, too.

Patrick ran his fingers over the jacket, letting them glide across the slick paper, then along the edges of the cover, down the spine, and around to the ends of the pages. So *many* pages! He turned the book over in his hands, letting the weight of it sink into his palms. Then, slowly, so no one would notice, he raised the book toward his face and breathed in the smell of all that paper. New. The book was really brand-new; it had never even been read. And it was his. A gift.

Patrick took a deep breath and slowly opened the cover. It was stiff, and crackled as it moved. The title, printed in dark, bold letters, jumped out at him. "THE SWORD IN THE STONE, BY T. H. WHITE."

Patrick almost shut the book. Letters like that demanded to be read. Demands made him nervous. But he steadied himself, and instead of closing the cover, he turned a page, and another.

Then he noticed the numbers at the top of each page, and without really thinking or plan-

ning, found himself turning and turning, looking for a certain number. . . .

There! A two, with another two right beside it.
He knew it—twenty-two. That was the number of
the page Celina had first read to him. How had
that part gone?

"There was a clearing in the forest . . ." Celina's
voice came from over Patrick's shoulder, making
him jump. He turned to see her leaning down,
her elbows on the back of the Reader's Chair, a
smile on her face. "Remember?" she said. *"There
was a clearing in the forest, a wide sward of moonlit
grass, and—"*

Patrick held up his hand like a cop at an inter-
section. Celina stopped and raised her eyebrows,
looking back and forth between the pages of *The
Sword in the Stone* and Patrick's face.

Patrick nodded, then returned to the book and
let his gaze run down page twenty-two, looking at
the words. It seemed almost easy to do with
Celina there.

Then he saw it. At the beginning of a line halfway down the page, tucked in a bit, "indented,"
like Mrs. Nagle always said. *There.* The word was
there, and behind it . . . *was. Was!* That was the
next word. Two words there on the page. He saw
them. He really looked at them, and he was OK.
No panic raced up his spine. The words were just

there like an . . . like an invitation. *There. Was.* Sure! *There was . . .*

Patrick went on. The next word he recognized, too. It was so little and simple—*a*. He'd known that one for years. And it fit together with the first two to make sense. Together with *there* and *was* he had the first three words of the line Celina had read to him so many times. *There was a . . .*

"There was a clearing in the forest," he whispered to himself, then looked at the next word. The letters C and L in front, then I-N-G at the back. That had to be *clearing*. And the next word must be . . . I-N . . . *in!* Then T-H-E. *The!* Yes! He knew that word. He'd seen it plenty of times before. F, O, and R were at the beginning of the next word. At the end was a T. Yep! That was *forest*. Just like Celina had read. Just like he knew by heart. *There was a clearing in the forest.* If he looked for the clues and thought about what made sense, he could read them smoothly, with no problems. *There was a clearing in the forest.* Letters together, not apart. Words together, not apart. It was a sentence. It meant something. It was part of a story, his favorite story. *There was a clearing in the forest.*

Patrick scanned the page, jumping from one word to the next. There was *the* again. And here was *in*. And that big word there . . . was it maybe

. . . maybe . . . *knight?* Yes, it was! Just like he'd seen Mrs. Romero write on the chalkboard once. He'd only looked at it for a moment, afraid that more might bring on the fear. But yes, that was it, there on the page. *Knight.* Patrick read the word, *"Knight!"*

Patrick turned the pages of *The Sword in the Stone,* rubbing them between his fingers, feeling the wonderful thickness of the paper, letting his gaze flow across the words, marveling at the variety of their length and shape, thinking about the wonderful story they could tell.

But he and Celina had never finished the book. How did it end? What happened to all of those characters he had come to care about? And what did a sword in a stone have to do with it all? Just who was Wart, anyway?

Patrick continued turning the pages of *The Sword in the Stone.* He had to find out. And now, for the first time in his life, he knew that he could. It would take time, and patience, but he could do it.

"Nice book, huh?" Celina said from over Patrick's shoulder.

Patrick looked up at Celina, but not before letting his eyes feast on the words before him for a moment more.

"Yeah," he said with a smile, "nice book."

Acknowledgments

When I was a kid, this is what I thought:

—Writers are strange beings born with "the gift."
—They never stew over spelling.
—They never forget the rules of punctuation.
—They never worry whether or not to start a new paragraph.
—And they never have to rewrite in better cursive because of picky fifth-grade teachers.
—They glide where I trudge.
—They soar where I end up flat on my face.
—For them writing is a piece of cake. Sitting alone in small attic rooms, they need only to stare out the gable window, and inspiration is sure to hit. Then they just write it all down, as simple as that! No help needed.

That's what I thought.

These days I think something different:

—All of the above is pretty much garbage, especially the part about writers needing no help.

So that's why I decided to publicly acknowledge (in no particular order) as many people as I could think of who helped (in a *wide* variety of ways) this story come to be. A big thank you to:

—Nan Phillips, M. K. Wren, Jean Naggar, Margery Cuyler, Kathy Short, Maggie Castillo, Terri Tarkoff, John Carpenter, Kathy Whitmore, Martin Nieves, Rick Meyer, Debbie Birdseye, the helpful folks at the Arizona-Sonora Desert Museum, Alan and Jane Flurkey, the teacher in Spokane, Washington, who told me a story of a magic book but never told me her name, Evelyn Gallardo, Alan Jacobs-Smith, Gitte Jorgensen, the librarians in the children's section of the Tucson Public Library, all the kids like Patrick I have known, or heard of, or read about, and anybody else who I—now being over forty—have happened to forget.

TOM BIRDSEYE
Tucson, Arizona, 1993

P.S. By the way, for those of you who are wondering—yes, the chuckwalla scene is based on a true incident. If you don't believe me, just ask John.

ABOUT THE AUTHOR

Tom Birdseye is the author of four novels for middle-graders—*Tarantula Shoes*, *Just Call Me Stupid* (both available in Puffin), *Tucker*, and *I'm Going To Be Famous*. He likes to hike and camp with his wife and two daughters. Tom Birdseye and his family live in Corvallis, Oregon.